Run Away Home

Run Away Home

PATRICIA C. McKISSACK

Scholastic Press / New York

Library of Congress Cataloging-in-Publication Data
McKissack, Pat, 1944–
Run away home / Patricia C. McKissack.
p. cm.

Summary: In 1886 in Alabama, an eleven-year-old African-American girl and her
family befriend and give refuge to a runaway Apache boy.

ISBN 0-590-46751-4 (hc)
1. African Americans — Alabama — Juvenile fiction. [1. African Americans —
Alabama — Fiction.   2. Apache Indians — Fiction.   3. Race relations — Fiction.
4. Friendship — Fiction.   5. Alabama — Fiction.
6. Indians of North America — Fiction.] I. Title.
PZ7.M478693Ru   1997
[Fic] — DC20   96-43673
CIP AC

10   9   8   7   6   5

Printed in the U.S.A.   37
First edition, October 1997
Design by David Caplan

Remembering Abraham Crossley,
the Sky in our family,
and
Thanking Nan and Peter for listening to
me read his story

Author's Note

My great-great-great-grandfather, Abraham Crossley, was a Native American. In the summer of 1977, when we visited southeast Alabama for a family reunion, my great-uncle told us the family legend of how the Crossley family had found a young Indian child in the woods. He was about seven or eight years old. The child grew up, married a black woman from the community, and supported his family as a carpenter. Of course, this story raised more questions than it answered.

For almost twenty years I have researched my paternal ancestor and bit by bit tried to piece together his life. Abraham might have been Seminole, he might have been Mobile, or he might have been Apache. I decided to investigate the possibility that he was an

Apache, because all the clues I had seemed to lead me in that direction.

In 1886, Geronimo and a band of thirty-nine Chiricahua Apaches, mostly women and children, surrendered to the United States Army after years of bitter warfare, under the condition that they would be sent to Florida for no more than a period of two years. Then they would be allowed to come back to the Southwest. Geronimo and his warriors were immediately put on trains and sent to Fort Pickens in Pensacola, Florida, where they were to be kept indefinitely. Their wives and children were held in eastern Florida. Meanwhile, other Apaches, even those who had served as scouts for the military, were rounded up and sent to Florida, too.

The Apaches remained as prisoners of war for two years, separated from their land, their families, and their lifeway. Then in May 1888, they were moved to Alabama, and in 1894 on to Fort Sill, Oklahoma. Coming west from Pensacola they would have passed through our old homeplace on the way to Mount Vernon, Alabama, which is thirty miles north of Mobile. It was during that transfer that a young boy could have escaped or somehow gotten lost when the train stopped for some reason. Based on the birthdates of his children, however, Abraham would not have been a very young boy as our family story suggests but at least fifteen years old.

Nothing is known about the African-American family who took Abraham in, but we know the times that shaped their lives. The 1880s were difficult years for the first generation of free blacks. Following the Civil War blacks were made full citizens with equal protection by the U.S. Constitution. But after President Rutherford B. Hayes withdrew federal troops from the south in 1877, southern states began the process of passing "Jim Crow" laws that segregated blacks from whites. Jobs and education were very limited, so many families ended up sharecropping, which was a continuation of slavery. The system proved to be unprofitable for both the landowners and the sharecroppers, so many whites and blacks left the rural South, seeking opportunities in northern factories or out West.

Some laws were designed to stop blacks from voting. For example, the states of Alabama and Mississippi instituted literacy tests to determine whether a person was qualified to vote.

The questions on the literacy tests had little or

nothing to do with a person's competency as a voter. "How many bubbles in a bar of soap?" and "How high is up?" are examples of two. Another test was to memorize the whole Constitution, which some blacks chose to do in order to keep their right to vote. When these tests were challenged in court, judges ruled that they were legal, because whites were required to take them as well.

In this way, blacks slowly lost the right to vote, and those who tried to resist the system were intimidated by violent white supremacy groups, even though such organizations had been outlawed by the Ku Klux Klan Act. These groups continued to terrorize the black community by burning schools and businesses, destroying property, and even murdering people. Seventy blacks were reported lynched in 1887 and sixty-nine were reported lynched in 1888.

This is the time Abraham would have come into the lives of the Crossleys.

Although I've been researching my paternal ancestry for almost twenty years, I am no closer to identifying Abraham's tribal affiliation than when I started. There are still too many loose ends for me to say with certainty that Abraham Crossley was an Apache, but there is compelling evidence based on what I've learned about Abraham to support the theory that he might have been.

This then is a work of fiction, based on the information I've gathered and the blending of two cultures. What I have not been able to find in fact, I have filled in with my imagination.

Happy reading.

Patricia C. McKissack
Chesterfield, Missouri 1997

Acknowledgments

I relied heavily upon the work of George Wratten, who was an actual army scout and a translator for the Apaches during their confinement. Some of the incidents in the book are based on Wratten's papers, especially those entries that dealt with how the mountain-dwelling Apaches fell victim to the heat and humidity of tropical Florida. I have also used old newspaper articles from the period, diaries, military records, and the work of Wooward B. (Woody) Skinner, who wrote *The Apache Rock Crumbles: The Captivity of Geronimo's People.* I'd like to thank Mary (Ching) Walters, of Pensacola, Florida, and Michael Darrow, historian of the Fort Sill Apaches, Fort Sill, Oklahoma, and all others who have helped me down through the years with my research. As always thanks to my editor, Ann Reit, my husband, Fredrick, and my family for their encouragement and patience.

CHAPTER 1

I walked behind Papa, listening to the dark, listening to the familiar sounds of the Alabama piney woods. A twig snapped, a night bird squawked, and an insect hummed. Somewhere in the distance a train whistle broke the silence and floated on the currents of the warm May breeze. That's strange, I thought. Quincy was at the crossroads, where tracks from all four directions intersected. I told time by the trains that passed through the town. The one I'd just heard was too late to be the morning westbound Mobile–New Orleans special, and too early for the 9:35 P.M. eastbound to Pensacola. It wasn't the *Flier* out of Mobile going to points north, and there was no southbound running anytime on Saturday. Where was this train headed? I wondered.

A shooting star raced across the heavens and I made a wish that one day I'd ride on a train to somewhere special — a big city maybe where ladies wore shoes all year long and carried umbrellas when it wasn't even raining. Mama had been all the way to St. Louis, but she didn't think too much of city life. Said she was glad to get back home. But she didn't discourage me, saying, "Hold fast to your dreams and one day you'll get to ride a train, see all the sights you want to see."

Hearing her, Papa always argued that it was the doers in the world who got things done. "Work, save yo' money, buy a ticket, and that's the way you'll ride — dreaming aine got nothing to do with it."

"But it's the dreaming-part that makes the working-part more tolerable," Mama usually answered.

I sometimes wondered how my folks ever got married to each other. Both were good people and they seemed to care about each other. That wasn't it. They were just so different. Just take what they call me. My name is Sarah Jane. Mama calls me Sarah and depends upon me to help her with the cooking and cleaning. Papa calls me Jane and says I'm his hunting and fishing partner.

Mama was a dreamer, who wished on stars, talked to flowers, thought nothing of hugging trees, and told the most wonderful stories her Indian grandmother had told. Mama was always taking in hurt things and mending their broken wings and legs, and then sending them on their way.

Papa, on the other hand, was a practical man, a former slave, whose life was centered on four things: food, clothing, shelter, and unquestioning faith. "A God-fearing man don't need luck and wishing on stars and such," he said on an average of three or four times a week.

I often wonder what I'm going to turn out to be. Is it possible to be a practical dreamer?

My thinking was interrupted by a low-hanging limb that snared my braids. It brought me back to the reality of the hunt.

How many times had Papa told me that the one thing standing between eating leather britches and rabbit stew was a little piece of attention. "A hungry hunter's got to be clearheaded in the woods — hear it, smell it, feel it," he'd said so many times, I could recite the words by heart. I'd been hunting with Papa since I was able to walk, and now that I was twelve, he had promised to let me shoot Sadie, his rifle. But I had to prove that I was responsible enough to handle a gun. Daydreaming wasn't responsible in Papa's eyes.

He paused, standing perfectly still, waiting. Suddenly, the full moon leaped from behind a cloud, spangling the darkness with a bright blue glow. A startled possum scurried from behind a log, but Papa had all ready spied it and was taking careful aim. The shot was sure to its mark as always.

"Good-sized possum, too," I said, checking out the catch.

Papa chuckled. "Cain't nobody fix the possum like yo' Mama. And with sweet potatoes . . . ummm."

"Better than dried string beans any day."

Then without warning, something big and furry sprang at Papa from out of the darkness, and he went sprawling to the ground. "Run, Jane," Papa called, scrambling for his gun. "A pan'ter's got me. Run!"

CHAPTER 2

I was scared, but not enough to leave Papa, I looked around for a big stick to use as a weapon. Then to my relief, the creature barked. Realizing it was Buster, the family dog, and not a panther, I let myself laugh, and the sound filled the hollow with a different kind of brightness. "It's just Buster, wanting to play, Papa," I said, wiping a laugh tear from the corner of my eye. I could tell by my father's expression that he wasn't tickled.

Papa hopped to his feet, adjusted his clothes, and recovered his hat from the ground. "Dang blasted dog, I aine somebody to be played with!" He slapped his hat against his leg and plopped it on his head, trying hard to salvage a small measure of pride. "Don't you dare lick me in my face!" he said, pointing a warning finger at Buster.

Hearing the scolding tone in Papa's voice, Buster knew he'd gotten on the wrong side of Papa again. So, with his head bowed low, the dog came straight to me, heeling like a well-trained dog of good breeding. His tail stayed lively, though, flipping and flopping from side to side.

"When will you ever grow up and stop being such a big puppy?" I whispered. Seeing Papa's disgust reminded me of how different things had turned out from the way Papa had planned. Somebody had thrown a sack of puppies in the river to drown, but one little pup had managed to survive. We'd found him down by the river — wet, sick, and half dead from starvation.

"Look at them feet," Papa had shouted all excited-like. "He's gon' to be a buster, for sho!"

Mama and I took to calling him Buster. Together we'd nursed the little throwaway through those first few days, spoon-feeding him warm milk every few hours, just like a baby. Buster grew into a big dog, built like a collie, but with a dark reddish coat of a redbone. But Papa's delight turned sour when no amount of training could turn Buster into a fine hunting dog. "Too wild, uncontrollable. Useless," he announced, dismissing Buster as a failure.

"Some creatures won't be controlled," Mama'd said. "Man who lived under slavery's cruel ways should know that."

"That sounds like that Indian grandma of yours talking. And besides, you aine got to remind me I was a slave and you wasn't." Papa'd fled to the barn to collect himself as he usually did when he and Mama crossed words. He'd come back to the house saying, "We can't 'ford to have nothing 'round here eating and sleeping that don't carry his own weight. We barely making ends meet as it is. That *dog* eats as much as a man and don't do one thing to earn his keep. Plain to me, he's got to go."

I could tell by the set of Mama's chin that she wasn't going to let Buster go so easily. "I had a hand in saving that dog's life," she'd said. "So I got something to say 'bout what happens to him." Mama rushed on, making her point fast. "I love that dog. Sarah is out here all by herself, no children to play with save Edna Mae Thompson, and she lives two miles away. If having Buster 'round can make Sarah happy, that's worth his keep to me."

Mama had persuaded Papa to change his mind, but first he had to save face. After retreating to the barn again, he didn't come back inside until the noonday meal. He'd poked up the fire in the fireplace, poured himself a cup of coffee, and leaned back in his rocker. "Just like I was thinking," he'd said at last. "Jane is out here all by herself. She might enjoy having that critter 'round. I 'spose the dog can stay."

That's how Mama had convinced my father that it was his idea to keep Buster. But at times like these, I wondered just how long Lee Andrew Crossman's patience was going to last.

Now, Papa bagged his possum and walked away in a huff, mumbling something about how Buster's name ought to have been Useless.

CHAPTER 3

Buster and I followed Papa, cutting across Grayson's Branch, a dry creek that could fill up in minutes during a storm. Buster lagged behind, nose to the ground, sniffing, then off again, chasing fleeing shadows. We emerged from the woods behind the Payne Chapel African Methodist Episcopal Church, and started down the east-west railroad tracks. It was only about a quarter of a mile to our farm, but between the church and the house, we came upon a train stopped on the tracks about a mile from the crossroads. It was facing west, so the train had come from the east — Pensacola or maybe even Jacksonville.

"This must be the train I'd heard from down in the hollow," I whispered to myself. The engine heaved big sighs. It looked like it was crouched and ready to spring into motion. Loud hissing escaped from its underbelly, followed by billows of steam. I moved closer to get a look at who was on that train. The moon cast enough light for me to see that four cars were filled with Indians — men, women, and children. There were old women with leathery brown skin, young men with dark, angry eyes, and there were children who looked poorly. They weren't Seminole like Mama's grandmother, or Creek, or any other Indian I'd seen before. There was a fifth car, which was for the soldiers, and two more for the soldiers' horses and other livestock.

Buster came charging out of the woods, asking questions in sharp barks. Papa went to the first soldier, who was standing by one of the coaches, and introduced himself and me.

I was glad Papa was more interested in finding out about the train and its passengers than paying attention to Buster's barking, which was getting louder and louder.

"Private Josiah Meeks, here," the soldier announced. "We got us a load of Apaches." The soldier spat tobacco juice to the side. "Meanest bunch of cutthroats ever walked on two feet," he added.

"Heard tell of them," said Papa, nodding his head. "Come through Mobile a while back; caused quite a stir then. Wasn't they being held over at Fort Pickens in Pensacola?" That's strange, I thought. Papa had never mentioned anything about Apaches before. But then again, he wouldn't talk about them unless they had something to do with food, clothing, or the farm.

"Yeah," the soldier hurried on. "I been guardin' them at Fort Pickens every sticky, hot day since they got here in October of 1886."

"Few months shy of two years," Papa put in. "They going back to where they come from?"

"The gov'ment aine never letting them go back to the Southwest," Private Meeks said, eyes narrowed. "Not in this life. We takin' them to Mount Vernon, 'bout thirty miles north of Mobile. Just waiting for word that the southbound tracks are clear. Next week, I'm out of this man's army, and I'm going back to Ohio and not coming south of the Mason-Dixon line again this 'side of judgment. Amen!"

A civilian stepped out of the fifth coach, dressed much like the Apaches. He had on a plain white shirt, a vest, brown trousers, and knee-high boots. Although he wasn't an Indian, he wasn't like the other white men. I was surprised when the soldiers addressed him as *Mister* Wratten, because he looked to be no more than twenty-one years old. And when Mr. Wratten snapped an order, the troops moved swiftly and unlocked and opened the third coach.

Through the opened window I heard Mr. Wratten speak to one of the Indians in what I supposed was Apache. Then he spoke again in English. "Come, Geronimo."

The face of the woman across from Geronimo was creased with concern. She jumped to her feet, saying something to Mr. Wratten I couldn't make out. It sounded like a question. A boy sitting next to Geronimo seemed to be worried, too.

Mr. Wratten answered in a calming and respectful voice. "Nothing bad is going to happen to Geronimo," he said, speaking to the boy. Then he turned to the woman, saying, "Lozen, we're moving him to the front coach, that's all." So Lozen was her name, I thought. The fact that she stood up to defend Geronimo when none of the other women did made me curious. There was something special about Lozen. I searched my head for the right word to describe her and I settled on strong, strong like Mama, determined.

Four armed guards came to take Geronimo on the short walk from the third to the first coach — one man in the front, two on each side, and one in the back. Though surrounded by soldiers Geronimo showed no signs of submission, no fear of his captors. Nobody had to tell me he was a person the soldiers had reason to fear. Yet, he didn't seem frightening to me.

Lozen and Geronimo were very much like the slaves Papa had told me about — the ones who showed no fear of their white masters — the ones the masters called "crazy" when they fought back or when they couldn't break their spirit.

I got a good look at the old warrior as he came down the steps of the coach. His head rested squarely on his shoulders the same way — yes, the same way Papa held his. There was a sureness in his walk and a straightness in his back that reminded me very much of Papa, yet the two men looked nothing alike. Geronimo was right at six feet, solidly built, muscular, unlike Papa, who was splinter thin, much taller, more leggy, yet strong, too, in his own way.

Buster's yelping grew louder. The soldiers seemed to bother him. "Shut that dog up or I'll . . ." One of the corporals leading Geronimo was ready to hit my dog with the butt of his shotgun. I gasped and drew back. Papa moved quickly, putting his body between us and the soldier.

"Where you goin', uncle?" the soldier said in a thick southern accent.

"That'll do, Jamison. At ease," said Mr. Wratten sternly. Just then Geronimo turned his head slowly and made a small gesture with his hands. Buster stopped barking instantly and sat calmly beside me, his tail flipping from side to side.

"Did you see that?" Private Meeks said. "I b'lieve what they say; Geronimo does have magic powers."

"Got nothing to do with magic," Papa said, tipping his hat and starting away. "He's just got a way with animals. My wife's got that gift. It's called kindness. It works better'n beating on a helpless critter," he added.

I was more interested in what they'd said about Geronimo. Did he really have magic powers? I looked back to take one last look at him, but that's when, over the shoulders of the soldiers, I saw the boy who had been sitting next to Geronimo leap through an open window and roll into the darkness. He never made a sound. It happened so fast I wondered if I'd really seen him. Meeks, Jamison, Wratten, and twenty other soldiers weren't thirty feet away from him, yet they hadn't seen or heard a thing. It was as though the boy was invisible . . . magically invisible. But no, I had seen him.

"Mr. Wratten."

"Yes," he answered. I started to tell what I had seen. But I stopped short when I looked into Geronimo's eyes. In that instant when our eyes met, I felt my inner self being lifted, higher and higher into the air . . . soaring on the wings of a great bird. I felt a gush of freedom that took my breath like a powerful wind. It all happened in a matter of seconds, then the spell was broken and Geronimo bounded up the steps and into the couch.

"Nothing," I said to Mr. Wratten.

Strangely I didn't feel frightened or confused. In his own magical way Geronimo had asked me not to tell what I had seen, and I didn't. I promised not to say a word to Mr. Wratten or the soldiers, not to Mama or Papa. I hoped Geronimo's friend would run far and fast — run away home — and be free.

CHAPTER 4

I was up half the night thinking about the Apaches, Geronimo, Lozen, and especially the runaway. Papa often told me about slaves who had tried to escape from The Pines, the plantation where he'd been born. Most of the time they were caught before they ever got started. Somehow the master always seemed to know. "He had spies," Papa said. "Somebody was always willing to tell on the promise of gettin' an extra piece of meat or a pair of shoes," he explained.

"I wouldn't have told," I always said.

"Let's hope you never have to be tested," Papa always replied. I'd been tested at the train, and I was proud that I hadn't tattled on a runaway.

But now in the quiet of my loft I had a chance to think on what I'd done. Private Meeks had said the

Apaches were cutthroats. According to Papa the slave masters sometimes said that runaways were bad people when they really weren't. I was a little bit worried. I hoped all the Indian boy was guilty of was wanting to be free. I couldn't blame him for that. I couldn't imagine being a prisoner or a slave — held in chains. People were meant to be free.

I always felt free, chasing the wind and playing with Buster in the woods and orchards and fields that made up our farm. No, *content* is a better word that describes my feelings. We all had our favorite spots on the place. Buster loved the woods, especially down by the creek where there were plenty of critters to chase. Papa was happiest when he got a chance to work with wood. I knew he was busy making a piece of furniture when I heard him whistling. Working the land took most of his time, so finding a moment to shape the wood was rare. The kitchen was Mama's special spot. She was the best cook in four counties and whenever there was a basket supper at church, Mama's pies were the first to be eaten.

But the loft was my special place, all mine. It was a small space under the roof, but it was a good room, full of strong feelings and bright memories.

It was just large enough for a bed, a table, a stool and a small chest. And even though it was miserably hot in the summer, I could always sit by the window and catch a breeze. Mama had let me decorate the loft with pictures cut from a catalog book, and I'd made blue-and-white gingham curtains for the small window that overlooked the barn and the fields and woods that made up our farm.

Our farm had been part of The Pines Plantation. After freedom, the white Crossmans had divided up the land and deeded twenty acres to each former slave, including Grandpa Amos Crossman. He had been the plantation carpenter — so good he'd been hired out by his master to make furniture for the governor's mansion. He'd taught Papa to be a fine carpenter, too, but after slavery there was no work for them. They had put away their saws and hammers and taken up the plow.

My loft was part of the two-room cabin Grandpa Amos and Papa had built, including every stick of furniture inside. Even though some black families had sold their land and used the money to move north or out west to start a new life, Grandpa Amos stayed and planted pecan trees and grew cotton.

When Papa married Mama, the loft had become their bedroom, and Grandpa Amos had added a bedroom off the big room and extended the porch all the way across the front. Just fine for sitting on hot summer nights. Grandpa Amos passed on, and I was born. The loft then became my room. I was lucky in some ways, not having to share anything with a brother or sister. My friend Edna Mae slept in the bed with three sisters, and the youngest one wet the bed almost every night. I would have gladly welcomed a sister or two to tell about seeing the Indian boy who jumped off the train. I'd have even been happy to have a brother, even though Edna Mae said her three brothers were awful. It sometimes seemed unnatural being an only child. Did that runaway Indian boy have brothers and sisters? Did they miss him? Did they get along? I wondered deep into the night.

Lying still on my bed, thinking in the darkness, I heard a train pass. Going to the window to get some fresh air, I saw Buster dart into the barn and then a shadow person go in behind him. It was the Indian boy. He hadn't gone anywhere. He was in our barn!

Everybody was up at rooster-crow-in-the-morning. But it was full day when I finally awoke. I could hear

Mama humming, making biscuits, and frying sausage. Hurriedly I splashed water on my face, dressed, and climbed down the ladder to the kitchen.

The kitchen, a large square room, was the heart of the house. We did all our living in that room. Mama was usually at the fireplace, which was used to cook, heat water, and warm the house in winter. A big round table took up most of the floor space. We ate our meals at it, but it was also Mama's worktable. She liked to sit straddling a bench, and lay her sewing out in front of her. I learned how to quilt and to read and write at that table. Papa's rocker stood by the fireplace, and there, after dinner, he read a passage or two from the Bible.

"I'm sorry I overslept," I said to Mama, grabbing the egg basket and rushing out the door before she could say a word.

Buster greeted me with several sharp barks, his tail slicing the air in big wide circles, in his language that meant good morning. "Hi, yo'self," I whispered, slipping past Papa, who was just outside the barn, putting a harness on Big Two, getting ready for his day's work.

"Morning, Miss Rich Lady," he teased.

I hurried to the chicken coop, quickly fed the chickens, then went inside to gather eggs while the fussy hens were eating. I had made up my mind that I had just been imagining things last night, until I only found six eggs; something was wrong. I looked around for signs of a fox. Behind the coop I found eggshells and a footprint — a human footprint.

I had seen the Indian. He had been here at the farm last night and eaten eggs. I remembered what Private Meeks had said about Apaches being cutthroats, and gasped. What had I done by not telling? Maybe the Indian was still nearby, watching and waiting for a chance to come in and kill us all! "Papa," I called out, fully intending to tell him everything. But I remembered something he had told me and I stopped.

Papa said runaway slaves were sometimes helped by conductors on the Underground Railroad — a group of people who led slaves from one safe hideout to the next, until they reached Canada. Was there an Indian Underground Railroad? Maybe people helped Apaches back to their home. I decided once more not to tell anybody what I'd seen, and I hoped and prayed that I'd made the right decision.

After milking January, our one cow, I started back

to the house to help with breakfast. Buster cut across my path, taking off down toward the main road, bounding through the grass like a buck deer. I could tell by his bark he wasn't chasing a rabbit or squirrel. From a distance, I could see a rider approaching on horseback.

"Somebody's coming, Papa," I said, setting the bucket of milk on the porch next to the eggs. Cupping my hands over my eyes to block the early morning sun, I made out that the rider was a man, but he didn't look like Mr. Patterson from down the road, and it wasn't Reverend Henry or one of the Thompson boys. The stranger was close enough now for me to tell he was a white man. That could mean trouble. Papa saw him, too, and reached for ol' Sadie, which was never far from him, night or day.

Chapter 5

White men on horseback had come to the farm before, telling Papa he'd better not try to vote. But Papa had voted anyway. The next day, somebody'd poisoned our first mule, Big One. It had taken a full year for Papa to save up enough to buy another mule. He got a special deal from a black family over in Barbour County, who had been burned out by the Knights of the Southern Order of Manhood. Everybody feared these men who did terrible things to people then hid behind hoods. They burned black houses, businesses, schools, and even lynched a few men. Rather than risk losing their lives, the black family decided to sell out cheap and move to the city — St. Louis, they say. Papa bought their mule.

Another time I remembered Mr. Charles Mayberry,

a rich white man, had come to our farm offering Papa the low, low price of two hundred dollars to buy it. Then he said Papa could stay on and work the land for a share in the profit. But Papa had refused. Anybody who knew Lee Andrew Crossman should have known no amount of money could buy him out. "I aim to keep this land. And, yo' sharecropping aine nothing but slavery with a new name."

I was proud of my father for taking that stand. But he paid a dear price for not caving in. Come planting time he wasn't able to get credit to buy seeds at Tucker's General Store. "Cash only," said Mr. Tucker, the owner. "Or you can get some white man to stand for you."

Papa knew that he was being boxed in. Once he got in debt and couldn't pay his taxes, he'd lose his property.

Sheriff Ray Johnson had overheard the conversation and stepped in, saying he would stand for Papa's seeds. "I owe you one, Lee Andy," he'd said.

Papa had helped Sheriff Johnson get elected by speaking for him among the black voters. Mama hadn't trusted Ray Johnson, saying, "His daddy was an overseer. His job was kicking, beating, and keeping slaves in their place. And an apple don't fall far from its tree."

Still, Papa had supported Mr. Johnson for sheriff despite Mama's warning. "I been knowing Ray Johnson since we were boys together. It aine that I trusts him so much. It's just that I'd rather go with a devil I know than a devil I don't."

Papa knew the sheriff wasn't helping him out of a clean heart. There was a reason, and that reason was clear to us all. But Papa's back was against the wall and he had to take the help. "A drowning man will grab a brick," he said. "If a good crop comes in, we'll pay off our debt to the sheriff and we'll be just fine."

Nobody had said it, but I was thinking it. "What if the crop failed?"

Now, looking out at the stranger coming toward us, I couldn't help but wonder what trouble might he be bringing?

Whoever it was, Buster took a liking to him and escorted the rider right up to the front porch steps. By that time I had identified him as the young man I'd seen at the train the night before. And I knew why he was there! A cold chill curled itself around my spine. I crossed my fingers and promised myself that I'd hold my secret no matter what.

"Morning to you," said Papa, remembering the man's face from the night before. "I'm Lee Andrew Crossman. We saw you last night."

"Yes, I recognized the dog," the man said, smiling broadly. "I'm George Wratten, scout and interpreter for the United States Army. You saw us taking the Apaches to Mount Vernon," the man said to Papa, extending his hand. Rarely had I seen a white man shake hands willingly with a black man. Mr. Wratten took off his hat and ran his fingers through his sandy brown hair. His eyes were always busy, taking in everything around him, never missing a thing. It was May, but it was hot and humid already. He wiped his face and neck with a large blue-and-white kerchief, then he slid off his horse. "I wasn't sure whose farm this was," he said, smiling real easy-like. "Glad to meet you again."

Mama had come out on the porch by that time. Papa introduced her and then me. Mr. Wratten tipped his hat and greeted us courteously. No, Mr. Wratten didn't act like most of the white men who lived in Alabama.

"Have any of you seen an Indian boy about fifteen or so around your place? He ran away while we were waiting for clearance on the eastbound tracks last night. Been looking for him most of the night. Hear anything, see anything?"

Mama and Papa shook their heads, but I shook mine the hardest, adding, "No, aine seen *nobody,* heard *nobody* at all." I couldn't look Mr. Wratten in the face.

"May I trouble you for some water, before I push on?" he asked ever so politely.

"Help yo'self," said Papa, handing him a dipper and adding, "is this here runaway dangerous?"

Mr. Wratten walked over to the well by the porch. "If threatened he could be," he answered.

"I'm about to put breakfast on the table," Mama put in. "Aine much, but you're welcome to share with us." To my surprise, the young man accepted. No. Mr. Wratten wasn't like any white man I had ever known.

I was glad he was staying, because I wanted to know as much as I could about Geronimo and the runaway, and now I'd get to find out from Mr. Wratten.

27

When Mama made biscuits, she always cooked ex-
tras to use for bread pudding at supper. Good thing,
because there was enough for the guest and nobody
was cut short.

I could hardly wait until Papa finished saying
grace, so I could start asking questions. "Who are the
Apaches?" I spoke right up as I passed the molasses.

Mr. Wratten spoke easily about the Apaches, like
he knew them well. "Apache is a name others gave
them. They call themselves *'Ndé,* which means
people."

"What about the boy who ran away? Who is he?"

Mama gave me a warning look. I had gone too far,
even for Mama, who was often criticized for allowing
me to dip into grown folks' conversations. "Pardon
my daughter," said Mama. "She's a magpie this
morning, talking and asking far too many questions."

Mr. Wratten didn't seem to mind, though. In fact he
wanted to tell us about the Apaches. He went right on
talking without answering my questions and that
suited me just fine.

"In his language his name means *He Looks At The
Sky,* but we all call him Sky for short. He grew up in
the Southwest Territory, the land we call Apacheria —

for centuries the home of Mimbre, Mescalero, Chiricahua, and other Apache groups. There among the sacred mountains they worshipped their god Ysun and practiced the customs that they call the lifeway. When intruders came and tried to take their land, whether they were Spanish, Mexicans, other Indians, or white Americans, the Apaches fought them harder and longer than any other Indians ever had. Many people died in those battles — many whites, many Indians, many Mexicans. Some of your people, even," he said, turning to Papa.

"Word tell 'round here that there were black soldiers out West." Papa passed the sausage. I noticed that Mr. Wratten didn't take any.

"Some Indians called them the Buffalo Soldiers because their hair was thick and coarse like that of the buffalo," he said. "They were some of the best fighters in the West."

The more Mr. Wratten talked, the more I didn't need to ask. I found out Sky was just three years older than me, but among his people he had passed the test to be an adult, a warrior, accepted as a full member of the male community, able to speak up in meetings and make decisions for himself. Mr. Wratten filled the morning with stories about Apache leaders named Mangas Colorados, Cochise, Victorio, and Geronimo.

"I was there when Geronimo and his thirty-nine people surrendered," Mr. Wratten said. "Sky was one of them. You see, the old warrior is a *di-yin,* which the Apaches believe is one who had been blessed with special powers, a visionary, a prophet. Geronimo looked into his power and saw that it was time to end the bloodshed."

I could tell Mr. Wratten admired Geronimo. Maybe it was because he had run the Mexican and United States armies ragged trying to capture him. Or maybe Mr. Wratten felt bad that the government had broken so many promises made to the Apaches and other Indians for years and years.

He told us that the government had sent Geronimo and his people to Florida as prisoners of war and rounded up those Apaches who were trying to live peacefully on the Fort Apache reservation and sent them to Florida to join those who were already there. "The government agreed their exile was only to be for two years, but . . ." Mr. Wratten's voice trailed off.

"The government promised my grandma's people

all kinds of things and went back on each and every one of them," Mama said.

Mr. Wratten eyed her curiously. "Mrs. Crossman, are you part Indian?" He wasn't the first person to ask that and with good reason. Her skin was dark, reddish brown. She had black oval-shaped eyes, high cheekbones, and straight black hair. Mama's grandmother was full Seminole from Florida. "My grandfather was a mulatto, a runaway slave from Georgia, who lived among the Seminoles. They were called Maroons. When the slaveholders got angry 'bout the runaways, they pushed for the soldiers to come take them back to their masters. But their own laws worked against them. During slavery times, black children were born under the same condition of their mothers," Mama explained. "My Grandma Jen was an Indian woman who married a runaway slave. All her children were born free, including my mama and then me. Grandma Jen bought her husband's freedom to keep him from being took back to his master. He was killed fighting with Osceola against Andy Jackson. So, I guess you might say, I'm a mixture of Afric', Seminole, and a little Scot-Irish if you digging for bones."

"Most Americans are mixtures of some sort." Mr. Wratten owned that his wife was Apache. "Any children we have will be Apache-English-French and a hint of Swede."

"I reckon that boy's folks must be worried sick about him," Mama put in.

"Sky's parents are dead, killed in a raid led by Mexicans. He has no other kinsmen. So, according to custom, he's under the guardianship of his headman, who is Geronimo, himself." Mr. Wratten looked at Mama with careful blue eyes. "Sky came of age under the guidance of Geronimo, so he's prepared to kill his enemies in ways you can't even imagine. Make no mistake about it, Sky is not a timid little boy. He's a Chiricahua Apache, quite capable of taking care of himself in any situation."

Papa passed the grits and changed the subject, asking Mr. Wratten where he was from.

"Wisconsin," he offered freely. "Took out on my own back in '79 — not much older than Sky. Worked in Arizona as a store clerk, then I was a packer. And for six and half years I was chief of scouts for the United States Army. Now I'm an interpreter for the Apaches in their confinement."

I was amazed that Mr. Wratten had experienced so much and had yet to see his twenty-fourth birthday. Papa must have gone on for fifteen minutes or more, talking about his cotton crop and pecan trees. It was hard for me to listen, because I was thinking about what Mr. Wratten had told us about Sky. I didn't think I was protecting a cutthroat, just a person like me who wanted to be free. But I still wasn't sure.

When Mr. Wratten had sopped the last of his biscuit in molasses and washed it down with hot coffee, he made quick his departure. We didn't get much company, and when we did, Mama was always sad to see them go. "I do appreciate your hospitality, Mr. and Mrs. Crossman. But I'll be on my way back to Mount Vernon now. No need hunting for Sky any longer. He's probably long gone."

"Long gone by now," I said, hoping with all my heart that Sky had hopped a train and was on his way home. "No more need to look," I added.

And Mr. Wratten tipped his hat and rode off. Whew! I was glad he had come, because he had answered a lot of my questions. But I was so glad I hadn't said anything that might put Mr. Wratten on to what I knew.

CHAPTER 6

Nothing much happened the rest of the day, but late that night a spring thunderstorm rumbled through the countryside. I was dreaming about Mr. Wratten accusing me of knowing about Sky and not telling him, when a clap of thunder woke me with a start. Lightning lit up the loft.

There was a time when I would have been scared and gone running to Mama. But as the storm moved overhead, I slipped to the window to listen to the music of the storm the way Mama had taught me to do. "Every thunderstorm has its own melody," she'd said. "No two storms ever sound the same." And it was true.

Lightning zigzagged across the heavens, writing a bright song. Thunder performed it in a big booming voice, while raindrops danced with the wind on the old tin roof. It was hard to imagine ever being afraid of thunder and lightning.

Even though it was just May, the loft was already stuffy. Another flash of lightning streaked across the heavens. That's when I saw him — first there, then he wasn't — as he slipped into the barn.

"I see you, Sky!" I whispered. Why hadn't he run away? Why was he still here? Then I realized Buster wasn't barking. If anybody came near our place, night or day, he barked. Why wasn't he barking now? I couldn't bring myself to say what I was thinking, but I had to find out.

Dressing quickly, I crept down the ladder into the kitchen. I took Sadie off the mantel where Papa kept it, then tiptoeing past Mama and Papa's bedroom, I eased out the door and hurried toward the barn. Buster met me at the barn door and I was relieved. Nothing bad had happened to him. He was yelping all excited, turning in circles the way he did when he'd cornered a rabbit and wanted to play with it, but the rabbit was too frightened to move. "What is it, Buster, a rabbit or a fox?" I said, trying to decide what to do.

Every now and then Buster got bitten by critters

that he cornered. Mr. Wratten had said Sky could be dangerous if he felt threatened. I didn't want Sky to think I was his enemy. I stood silently, straining to hear the slightest movement. The barn was dark, but I could feel the presence of another person, the way Papa had taught me to feel the presence of a critter I was hunting. Sky was in the darkness. I thought I heard his heart beating, then I realized it was my own heart pounding.

Good sense told me to go back in the house and get Papa. But, I'd come this far with the runaway and I was bound to see it through. I leaned Sadie against the door and held up my hands to show I meant no harm. Mr. Wratten had said he was an interpreter for the Apaches. I hoped Sky knew enough English to understand me.

"I know you're in here," I called. "Your name is Sky and you're an Apache. I saw you jump off the train the other night, but I didn't tell then. I won't tell now."

Lightning flashed and I used the second of light to see as much as I could. Nothing. Sky seemed to be part of the darkness. "I want to help you," I whispered. I tried to think how it might feel being a runaway slave, trapped in a barn miles and miles away from home. "You'll be safe and dry here in the barn for the night. But you need to know that Mr. Wratten has been here looking for you. He said he was going back to Mount Vernon."

Still no answer. I don't think I expected one. "If it was me, I'd jump one of the trains that runs through here and be long gone by morning." I backed out of the doorway and picked up Sadie as I passed. "I'm going now. Oh, by the way, Buster won't hurt you, unless you try to harm a hair on anybody's head in this family," I added just for good measure.

Tracing my steps going back into the house, I put the gun up and climbed back to the safety of my loft. When I'd changed into dry clothing, I stretched out on my bed. My whole body shook. Hugging myself with my own arms, I closed my eyes and tried to calm down.

At last, the storm passed over and stars twinkled behind fast-moving clouds. I lay awake the rest of the night, watching and wondering about all that had happened. A train whistle blew in the distance. For the first time I prayed that somebody else was on it. "Run Sky. Run away home."

CHAPTER 7

Sky didn't run!

In fact he was still in the barn the next morning when I went in to milk January. I'd never seen Sky up close, yet it felt like I'd known him forever. Mr. Wratten had said among his people he was considered a man, but staring at him lying in the straw he looked like a boy to me. I put my arm next to his. We were the same shade of brown. He had a pierced earring in his ear. A boy with an earring? I rubbed the small scar on my leg — the one I'd gotten from falling on a sharp stick. How had he gotten the crescent-shaped scar on his forehead? I touched the dark shoulder-length hair that framed his round face. Like mine, his hair felt thick and coarse, but his was straight and mine was curly.

Suddenly his dark eyes blinked open, and he grabbed my hand. I didn't have time to be scared. He said something in Apache, all the while gasping for breath. Something was wrong with him.

I touched his forehead. "Sky, you're burning up with fever."

He wanted something. He spoke in Apache. I shook my head. "Do you know English?"

"Water," he managed to say through parched lips. "Water," he said again, struggling to get to his feet.

"You need help." I tried to hold him up, but his legs were limp and lifeless.

Sky groaned.

"Come on." Where was I going to take him? By that time Buster had alerted Mama, who had rushed to the barn. The decision was no longer mine to make alone. Good that it was Mama and not Papa, though.

With one glance Mama understood who Sky was and what was going on. She reacted with a quickness. "Did you know this boy was out here and didn't speak up?" she asked as we half carried, half dragged Sky into the house and made up the sickbed. We hung quilts over a clothesline to partition off the space from the rest of the room, then laid a pallet of quilts. Glad for somebody else to know, I told Mama everything from when I'd seen Sky escape to finding him this morning. "Are you mad at me?" I asked.

"Well, I can't fault you for wanting to help somebody in need. But I'm not happy that you didn't tell me. You heard Mr. Wratten say this boy could be dangerous. What were you thinking of, taking this on by yo'self?"

Guilt was choking me and tears stung my cheek, but I managed to answer, "I-I-I just didn't want to be a tattler like the ones that used to turn in the runaways during slavery time."

"Slavery time is over. This is now, young lady. You might have gotten us all in trouble here. We'll talk about this later," she said in her no-nonsense voice. "Right now, I need help getting his shirt off."

When we pulled the shirt over Sky's head, Mama sucked in her breath and clicked her teeth. I covered my mouth to keep from screaming. He was covered with what looked like hundreds and hundreds of mosquito bites. He had scratched them and they had formed sores.

"Swamp fever," Mama whispered. By then, the boy was shaking with chills. We covered him with quilts, and wrapped his hands with strips of cloth so he couldn't scratch and infect himself more.

"Boil water for sassafras tea," Mama snapped an order. "We've got to drive the impurities out of his body."

Mama began humming, the way she did when she was deep thinking, worried, or unsure. "I need quinine," she said. "Run get yo' daddy."

Turning around, I ran right into Mr. Wratten, who looked larger than life, framing the doorway. "I have some quinine in my saddlebag," he said. Right away, I guessed Mr. Wratten had not gone back to Mount Vernon, but had hung around, suspecting that maybe Sky was hiding out at our place, or we were hiding him. He'd probably seen us carry Sky into the house and come to get him. Seeing how sick Sky was, Mr. Wratten's face softened with concern. "Looks bad," he said. "If I try to take him back to Mount Vernon, he'll never make it."

"Leave him here, then," I said, knowing I was speaking out of place, getting deeper and deeper into trouble with Mama. But I couldn't help myself. I went right on talking. "Mama knows Indian ways; she can help him."

Mr. Wratten looked to Mama for her consent. Sky coughed and moaned. She mopped his forehead with a cool cloth. "I might can't save him," she said. "But I can try."

Mr. Wratten studied on the idea, shifting his weight from foot to foot. "So many Apaches died in Florida," he said, looking beyond Mama to some place in his past. "They're a mountain people, used to dry, cool weather." He mumbled something about the damp climate that seemed to sap the life right out of the Apaches. He was talking more to himself than us.

"Can the boy speak English?" Mama asked. "That might make things a whole lot easier later on."

"Sky speaks Apache and Spanish," he answered. "But he can manage English better than most. He learned it mostly by listening and from a few nuns who used to come several times a week to teach those who were interested. Sky is interested in everything."

Mr. Wratten sighed deeply. "Sky will be better off here for the time being," he said. "I guess I'll just say I couldn't find him."

I felt relieved. "If he doesn't make it," he added, "wire me that *the quilt is torn.* If he makes it, wire me that *the quilt is ready,* and I'll come get him. Don't let Sky know I've been here or he'll run again." Mama agreed.

Following Mr. Wratten out to his horse to get the quinine, I asked, "Why did Sky run?"

"Sky is the first Apache who has run away. I don't think he wants to go to Carlisle School for Indians up in Pennsylvania. And I can't say as I blame him. Most Apaches who go there come back home in a coffin. As many of them die of homesickness as they do from diseases."

I had many more questions, but it was not the time to ask. Mr. Wratten was gone by the time Papa came in from the fields for noontime meal.

When Papa didn't smell anything cooking and saw who we had made the sickroom for, he commenced to fussing. "What are you thinkin' 'bout, Georgianne? How could you bring trouble to our front door like this? Mr. Wratten was just here lookin' for this boy, and here we got him in our house, takin' care of him."

"He's sick and needs our help," Mama said. "And besides," she added, "Mr. Wratten knows he's here and asked me to care for him 'til he gets better."

"Aine it enough 'round here to do, besides taking on a sick boy, somebody we don't even-now know. What business is it of ours?"

Mama had started a pot to boil some rice. But she stopped and raised the wooden spoon as if she planned to use it as a weapon. "Lee Andy, you the one always talkin' 'bout how you s'posed to love yo' neighbor as yo'self. What meaning is in them words?" Mama asked.

Right away, Papa fled to the barn. Within the half hour he came back, Bible story in hand.

"I'm reminded here of the parable of the Good Samaritan who took care of a stranger he found 'side the road. It is right that we should take care of this poor soul who is in need. I've made up my mind, now. So, don't try to talk me out of it."

"Yes, you're right, Lee Andy," Mama said.

I turned away so Papa wouldn't see me smiling as I spooned hot tea into Sky's mouth.

CHAPTER 8

Getting Sky through the night took a powerful lot of doctoring. I sat by his bedside, hoping some and praying some, always helping Mama by fetching and carrying whatever was needed. Sky tossed and turned, and yelled out in his feverish sleep, calling Geronimo's name, and mumbling words in Apache. "Fight," I whispered to him. "Fight to stay alive. Don't give up."

Mama burned herbs and called upon her grandmother for guidance. And then she rattled her bag of bones over his body and sang a song her father had taught her. Say he had learned it from his Afric' mama. I put the words in my head, so as not to forget them.

Tak me hum mi hum mi hum
Tak me hum mi hum mi hum
Tak me hum mi hum mi hum
Mi hum fu wa fu wa mi hum.

All through the night I rubbed Sky's arms and legs with a soothing paste Mama'd made from dried roots.

Papa didn't hold with Mama's bag of bones and her incantations. But he had come to reason long ago that Mama's ways — though strange to him — had good results. "You know a tree by the fruit it bears," he said with conviction. "Good trees yield good fruit. Bad trees don't. It's as simple as that." He helped out in his own way, reciting Psalms and peering into the sickroom, offering a word of encouragement now and again.

Sky's fever broke early the next morning, shortly before the southbound rumbled through Quincy. But he wasn't out of the woods yet — far from it. On the third day, his breathing settled into a steady rhythm as his body stayed cool. "He'll make it," said Mama, giving her head a quick nod, the way she did when she felt triumphant. Strengthened by her success, Mama stopped humming and sang a happy tune while preparing breakfast.

But I was bone tired because I hadn't slept more than a few hours in days. Now that it looked like Sky would live, I yawned and stretched and dragged into the kitchen. "Put a little life in your step," Mama said in a lively way. "You're too young to know what tired is."

Yes I do, I wanted to say, but dared not be that sassy. I was forever getting my legs switched for talking back, talking out of turn, or just plain talking too much. When I'm all grown up, I thought, I'm going to say what's on my mind. But that was a ways off. As far as I knew I was still on the wrong side of Mama, even though she hadn't mentioned anything to Papa about my part in Sky's escape. I decided it was best not to rile her. So I kept my mouth shut and took joy in knowing we would not have to wire Mr. Wratten that *the quilt is torn.*

Buster met me at the door, yelping all kinds of questions. I explained everything to him, putting in all the details about how we'd saved Sky's life. He listened, head cocked to one side as if he understood everything I was saying. "Buster, I'm so glad I've got you to talk to," I said. "You're a good dog, no matter what Papa thinks."

The smells of Mama's kitchen must have awakened Sky. He was sitting bolt straight in the bed, looking wild-eyed and frightened when I brought a plate of food to him. He asked something in Apache. When I shook my head to show I didn't understand, he switched to English. "Where is this place?" he asked, trying to get up, but he was too weak.

Putting my hand on his shoulder, I smiled, saying, "Here, lie back down, before you . . ."

Sky pulled away and his first words to me were, "I don't know you!" He snapped at me in very clear English, "I don't know you." This time, I snatched my hands away like I'd touched a sleeping alligator by accident. He tried to sit up, but once more he flopped back down on his pallet.

"I was just trying to help," I said, feeling put out. The past few days, I'd imagined a lot of things about Sky, but I never expected him to be an Un-person. In my way of thinking, an Un-person was one who was unkind, ungrateful, unpleasant, unfair, un-anything.

The patient wasn't any nicer to Mama. When she

tried to get him to eat, he shoved it away. "No pig meat," he said, looking down in disgust.

Maybe the fever had addled his brain, I thought.

"Eat a few grits, then," Mama insisted. "You need to build up your strength again. You're still sick."

"I am not sick!" he scoffed. Sky would have nothing to do with us. He pulled the sheet up to his chin, and refused everything we offered him. By then I was close to tossing the food on his head. Just then Papa came in.

Papa introduced everybody by name, including himself. "This is my family." Sky shook his head, never taking his eyes off Mama, who stood at the foot of the bed. "Son, you're 'mongst the living this morning, 'cause of the Good Lord working through my wife and my daughter." Sky seemed to be hanging on every word Papa said. "Now, let's get this understanding," Papa went on. "As long as you're in this house, you'll treat them with respect or I'm gon' know why. Clear?"

It took me back when Sky's whole attitude changed in a hurry — I mean, right now. He commenced to eating, shoving down three helpings of grits, eggs, and biscuits — but he still wouldn't touch the pork.

He was still an Un-person, I decided — ungrateful! But I remembered one of Papa's favorite sayings. "Tote the load of another person 'fore you pass judgment." So I put myself in Sky's shoes. He had awakened in a strange man's house and bed with that man's family attending to him in a very personal way. Maybe he wasn't being rude, but waiting until he had been welcomed by the head of the household — Papa. Somehow Sky had gotten a welcome in Papa's words — the permission he needed to feel comfortable with us. I may have been all wrong, but my reason made good sense to me.

CHAPTER 9

Sky improved a little each day. Still, he was weak and slept a lot. Mama said it would take him a while to build up his strength. Even when Sky was awake he didn't talk much. I had a million and one questions I wanted to ask him, but dared not, because Mama had forbidden me to, and Sky wasn't the easiest person to get to know. I had the feeling he didn't trust us, and he would have been long gone if he hadn't been so sick. Mama and Papa kept their distance and warned me to do the same.

"Let him be. He needs rest. And don't you go gettin' attached to that boy, 'cause he'll be leaving soon," she said one morning while braiding my hair.

Get attached to Sky? That wasn't likely to happen.

So far, Mama hadn't told Papa how I'd protected

the runaway, but she made me promise that I wouldn't warn Sky this time. "He'll run again," she said, "and the authorities might make it hard for us." In a few days we were going to wire Mr. Wratten that *the quilt is ready.* If Sky had been halfway nice, I might have helped him, but Mama didn't have to worry about me helping him ever again.

Buster on the other hand had taken a liking to Sky. When Sky was able to come out on the porch for the first time, Buster came bounding up the steps, his tail wagging from side to side, begging for a hug. Sky spoke to him in Apache and Buster's ears perked, like he understood.

"He's mine," I said. "We call him Buster," I added, knowing all the time that they had already met. Sky never said a word to me but went on talking to Buster. As Papa was fond of saying, "You catch more flies with sugar than bitters." So I tried not to let Sky turn me into an old sour mouth — but he was pushing.

Sky had been with us about three weeks when one Saturday morning, Papa hitched Big Two to the wagon. He and Mama were going into town. Mama looked so pretty in her blue-and-white-gingham dress and crisp white apron, but she was as barefooted as the day she was born. Soon as the weather cleared Mama and I came out of shoes. After a rain, I loved the feel of red Alabama clay mud oozing through my toes.

I figured Papa would wire Mr. Wratten while they were in town. "The quilt aine ready today," Mama whispered, guessing what I was thinking. "That boy aine quite well enough this week. Next week maybe."

I ran to get Mama's basket for the few things she'd pick up at the store, even though it wasn't going to be much. Sheriff Ray Johnson had stood for Papa to run a bill at Tucker's General Store until harvest time, but Mama didn't trust him and only bought what she had to have — and not a peppermint candy stick more.

Buster and I ran alongside the wagon until it reached the outer road. "Remember your word," Mama said. I waved until the wagon turned out of sight, then I turned back toward the house.

Mama had washed and ironed Sky's clothes, and he had dressed by the time I got back to the house. He was tying on his headband.

"Why do you wear just one earring?" I just had to know.

"My grandmother pierced my ear when I was born," he said matter-a-factly. "It drove out any evil spirits that might have entered my body at birth. I never take it out."

"Then do girls get their ears pierced, too?"

"Why are you so full of questions today?" he said sternly. "Your mother and father are good and wise people. They do not push, push, push for my thoughts. You would be wise to do the same thing."

I wanted to say it was because they didn't want to know him, but I held my tongue and found something to do on the porch. I wanted to like Sky, but he made it so hard.

He came outside, but his legs were still unsteady-like, so I offered to help him down the steps. "Lean on me," I said, "until you're stronger."

"Lean on you, Little Bush?" he replied, with a raised eyebrow. "You may snap in two."

"I can hold *you* up," I said, lifting my chin, trying to make myself look taller. Still, Sky stood two heads over me, but he was slender, so I figured I could make good on my boast. "I'm stronger than you think!"

"A stream that babbles is not very deep," he said, sounding an awful lot like Papa. Thing is, he wasn't my father so I didn't have to put up with his sayings. Once more I held my tongue, but it was getting harder and harder to do.

After helping Sky into the yard I sat in the shade of the large live oak, but he chose to sit in the full sunlight. With arms stretched out and palms up, he sucked air into his lungs and exhaled slowly — very slowly. His eyes seemed to laugh as they moved from tree rustling, to bird on the wing, to rabbit running, to bee buzzing, to wind stirring. He took it all in like a cool drink of water. I thought how peaceful he looked, how peaceful I felt watching him.

The spell was broken when Buster came charging in, greeting first one then the other, with barks, and wiggles, and big juicy licks across our faces. Sky hugged him and buried his face in his fur.

"Buster led you here the night you ran away, didn't he?" I said, rushing on to add, "Did you hear me that night in the barn? I really didn't tell anybody that I'd seen you jump off the train, honest."

I waited for Sky to say something, but he didn't — nothing — no *thank you,* or *that was nice of you, Sarah Jane* — nothing. He just looked straight ahead and seemed to ignore me.

That did it! I leaped to my feet and put my hands on my hips. "What's wrong with you?" I shouted. "Can't you see all I'm trying to do is be nice? I guess not, because you're too — too snippity!" And I stormed away, angrily.

CHAPTER 10

Papa was up bright and early and ready for church the next day. "Would you be interested in going to worship with us this morning?" Papa said to Sky.

"No," he answered bluntly. I could have told Papa not to even bother asking.

Mama agreed that she would stay in the house with Sky while Papa and I went to church. We weren't gone that long, but when we got home, we heard Sky and Mama laughing and talking like they had known each other for a long time. I looked at Sky, unable to believe that he was laughing. I was beginning to think Apaches couldn't laugh or had forgotten how. Then I looked at Mama, equally as amazed. The expression on my face must have reminded her of her own words. *Don't get attached . . .*

"How was service?" she asked, changing the subject from what she and Sky had been talking about. I wondered what *had* they been talking about that made Sky act so pleasant.

Papa told Mama all the church news — who was there, what the choir sang, who was on the sick and shut-in list, and what the sermon was about. "Reverend Henry preached from Genesis to Revelations, even though he said he was gon' talk about Paul. Oh, by the way," he added, "Founder's Day is coming up in a month or so. The committee's asked Professor Booker T. Washington from Tuskegee School to speak to us."

Mama nodded her approval. Then she asked about the local news. "I aine up on all that gossip," Papa said, laughing, leaving me to fill in those details.

"Mr. Lath Jones is back from Tuskegee School," I told her. "The term is over, but he can't wait to go back. He went on and on 'bout how fast the school is growing under the leadership of Mr. Booker T. Washington." I showed Mama a handbill Mr. Jones had passed out, telling about all the opportunities that were open to black students at Tuskegee. I put the handbill in my pocket because it had writing on it, and I could practice my reading with new words.

Mr. Jones made Tuskegee sound like a place I might want to go to, but Mama would have to be convinced. It wasn't that Mama was against education. Most everything I knew she had taught me, 'cause Miss Daisy's School for Colored Children was only open three months out of the year — when children weren't needed to work in the fields. Anybody who wanted to go further had to leave Quincy. And that's what Mama didn't like. "There should be a decent school right here in Quincy," she argued. "We ought not have to send our children far 'way to get an education."

There were schools up north for colored girls, but Mama wouldn't dream of letting me go there. "No chile of mine will go off and come back home looking down her nose at her people, too good to be with us. No indeed." Truth is, Mama couldn't bear to let me leave her, me being the only child and all. Maybe she'd think differently about Tuskegee that was just up the road. I sure hoped so. Besides, no amount of schooling could make me look down my nose at anybody, least of all Mama.

While I was thinking about school, Papa had his mind on something close to his heart — the right to vote. Over the past year, the Knights of the Southern

Order of Manhood had been threatening people who tried to vote, including him. With elections coming up in the fall, the Knights had ridden through the countryside, wearing hoods over their heads, burning barns and houses of anybody who tried to register. Papa called them cowards.

"They trying to keep us black folks from voting again," Papa said. "Lath Jones say that 'fore they'll let him vote, he's got to recite the whole Constitution by heart, every word. That can't be legal, and if it is, it ain't right. I tell you, things aine looking good for us."

Mama agreed, adding that half the people who were trying to stop the colored people from voting didn't believe in the Constitution themselves. "Otherwise they wouldn't be up to such devilment," she said.

While Papa finished telling Mama his ideas, Sky slipped quietly from the house and headed toward the woods. Buster followed him, and I followed them both. Just before going into the woods, he turned and shouted, "Go back. Why are you following me?"

"I can go where I want to on this property, and you can't stop me. This is my home and you're a guest here! You should start acting like it!" And I threw my head back and strutted away, leaving Sky to think on that for a spell.

To my surprise, Sky found me down by the creek. "Little Bush," he began, "it was you who didn't tell the soldiers. It was you who saved my life. I am happy with that. But I can't put a 'Indaa in my heart," he said. "That would be foolish. You are the enemy."

"Enemy?" I shouted in disbelief. "You think of us as your enemy?"

"All who are not Apaches are the enemy," he said. "You are not Apache."

"Mr. Wratten is not an Apache and he isn't your enemy," I said.

"He is shik'ine, a brother."

"Well, the way I see it, you've got a whole lot of people who aren't Apaches seeing after you. So you just better start thinking about who's your enemy!"

Sky looked at me with piercing black eyes. "I will not be a snippity no more," he said.

I couldn't help but smile. "I promise, no more push, push pushing for your thoughts either." We had found something to agree on and so we shook hands. Buster jumped up and put his paws on top of our joined hands and gave us each a good lick.

Chapter 11

I hadn't been truthful with Sky. And it was bothering me. We were going to do him harm and turn him into Mr. Wratten as soon as he was well. After another week passed, Sky was fine, but none of us wanted to see him leave.

I helped Mama take down the quilts that had made the sickroom, wash them, and put them away until they were needed again. Sky had slept outside all week, where he seemed to be most comfortable. He'd found a piece of hickory and was using Papa's tools to make a bow and arrows.

Although Sky never spoke the words thank you, he expressed his gratitude in so many thank-you ways. If a fence needed mending, he mended it. If Big Two needed feeding, he fed him. If a hole needed digging, he dug it. This pleased Papa. But Sky flat out would not do a chore that he considered woman's work. I couldn't get over the way he watched me struggling with a bucket of water and wouldn't offer to help, saying, "Less water would make it easier to carry."

"That is his way," Mama told me when I complained. "We can't expect him to change who he is to suit us. That's what's wrong with those schools that try to de-Indian his people."

In spite of herself, Mama had grown fond of Sky, too, and Sky was slowly allowing himself to smile more — and even talk more, too.

One day, while he was working on his bow and Buster lay between us, his tail thump, thump, thumping against the wooden floor, Sky turned to me and said, "Yes."

"Yes? Yes what?"

"Girls can have their ears pierced."

We both laughed. I couldn't be sure, but I felt that Sky was giving me permission to ask him a few things. And so I did.

Since the first night I'd seen the Apaches, I'd been curious about the woman who had risen to defend Geronimo.

"Who is Lozen?" I asked.

"Lozen," he began, still filing away on the wooden bow, "is sister of Victorio." I had heard Mr. Wratten talk about Victorio, so at least I knew who he was. "She is a war woman," Sky continued, "one who is equal to anyone in battle. She fought with her brother until he was killed, then she rode with Geronimo and she has great powers. I rode with her against the Mexicans and the whites. She was with us when we surrendered."

Lozen reminded me of a story Papa had told me about Harriet Tubman, a slave woman who had been a conductor on the Underground Railroad. Papa said she stood no taller than me, but she was strong and brave. She even served as a spy for the Union Army during the war.

Suddenly Buster took off down the path, chasing some critter he had no plans to hurt. "Most people don't understand him, because he's so wild," I said.

"There is a difference between what is wild and what is free," Sky said softly.

I knew he was thinking about his own people. They had been called wild because they fought so hard to stay free. A terrible war had been fought so we black people could be free. That should have included Indians, too. Now that I had gotten to know Sky, it bothered me that we were doing what all the others had done to his people. I didn't like it, but my word is out to Mama.

My mind returned to Lozen, and I imagined myself riding with her, the wind at my back, the sun in my face.

"What time of year is this?" Sky had to ask me three times to bring me out of my wonderful daydream. "Your mind is in too many places," he said.

"There you go, sounding just like Papa," I said. "It is June of 1888," I added. Clearly that meant nothing to him. Looking for a better way to answer, I decided to show him the farm. He had seen it, but not through my eyes.

First we went to the kitchen garden where Mama had set out turnips, collards, beans, corn, tomatoes, okra, sweet potatoes, goobers, and peppers. "We'll eat out of this garden all summer, then we'll can or dry a lot of it come fall."

"What's a goober?" he asked.

"Goobers are peanuts, and just wait 'til you taste them." Sky knew a lot of the foods I named, and even told me how his mother had used peppers and corn to make his favorite dishes.

Next we visited the orchards, where I showed him peach, apple, and pecan trees. "My grandpa planted these trees when he got this land. Papa says you don't plant a pecan tree for yourself, but for your grandchildren, because it takes near about fifteen years for it to bear nuts."

Sky touched the bark of the tree as if he expected it to tell him an old secret. I touched the tree, too, but it said nothing — nothing that I could hear.

Then I took him to the fields. The cotton was up waist high. "You know it's summer when the days are long and hot — but not hot-hot yet."

"Ah," he said, "the time of Little Leaves." I could see him putting the idea of summer in his head to use later, and I was doing the same with his words.

Sky quickly shifted the subject, as if an idea had just come into his head. "You say this time is Little Leaves, but when I was sick I felt hot like the time of Many Leaves, then I was cold and shook like it was the time of Ghost Face."

I understood that to mean that since it was late

spring, why had he felt hot like it was summer and then shivered like it was winter. He went on, saying, "I was burning like a fire inside. Your mother must be a powerful *di-yin* to have put out this fire."

"Those were chills you were having," I explained. "You were eaten up by mosquitoes and they gave you a bad fever; we call it Swamp Fever."

"Mosquitoes? You mean the little fire bugs that make you claw at your body? No. I think it was the fish," he said, struggling to get to his feet. The words seemed to make him nervous.

"Long time ago, my people were sick," Sky began. "They had terrible fever, just like me. The *di-yin* took them to the river for a cure, but they all died. The family members were angry with the *di-yin* and believed he was a witch. They were about to kill him when they noticed that the dead people had turned spotted like the fish in the river. Fish are not fit to eat."

"You gon' get mighty hungry 'round here," I said, laughing. Sky's face darkened and I realized he was very serious. So I became serious, too. "I meant no harm, Sky, but I eat fish all the time and it don't hurt me." Then, looking for an understanding, I added,

"Maybe your people got a hold of some spoiled fish. Now, that'll turn you against it forever. But when fish is fresh, it won't hurt you none."

Sky was not convinced. He seemed really upset when he talked about it. "In Pensacola they say your words. We know better and we try to resist, but our bellies cry out for food. So we eat the fish and our bodies weaken, and some of us cough and throw up blood, then we die." I could hear shame and anger in his voice. His expression was the same as Papa's was when he talked about being hungry during slavery times. That's why our smokehouse stayed full. Papa never wanted me to know that kind of hungry feeling.

As we walked, a hawk screeched overhead and a squirrel ran for cover. Sky stopped to touch other things, to smell them along the way. When we found a nest of chickadees that had fallen out of a mulberry bush, he gently put the nest in a safe spot off the ground.

"What was it like where you grew up?"

"In our homeland our families lived together in . . ." He looked for a way to explain it to me. He began again. "We lived in groups where the women built our houses, and the men hunted. "The Mexicans called them *rancherios*. That is not our word. The closest word to ours is just *home*. We grew corn. The men made their bows and mended their boots, and the elders taught us the important stories. Now that is no more. I was born at the time of Little Eagles, when the women gathered the stem from the yucca plant."

When I didn't know what a yucca plant was he drew it in the dirt with a stick.

During Many Leaves, Sky said he and his mother had gathered mescal and wild onions and made a stew. He sniffed the air, trying to remember the smell. "Large Leaves is the time of heat — you call it summer — when wild seeds and grains were gathered," he said, "and the women boiled them into stew and made flour for breads." Thick with Frost is harvest time for fruit. "Everybody in the rancherio hunted for wild berries, and nuts, which we ate raw or dried for later. Nothing is better than bread and honey," he said. Then came Earth Reddish Brown and just as I'd guessed, Ghost Face — winter. "That's when nights grow long and the Spirit of Darkness and Death walks the earth," he explained. "The knife of cold cuts

69

through to our bones and nothing can warm us, not even fire."

When he had finished, I felt the chill of a dark winter's night and knew exactly why the Apaches called winter Ghost Face. "The seasons of Apacheria are much more interesting than our January, February, March, April, and so on," I said.

By then we had reached the woods. We looked up at the stand of cypress, pine, oak, hickory, and cedar. I paused and so did he. We both saw the buck deer at the same time. We stood very, very still. It sniffed the air, then darted through the brush and disappeared. "You do know how to be quiet at the right time," Sky whispered, then flashed a big toothy smile. "What's that mean?" I asked. Sky walked ahead, never bothering to answer. "You really make me mad when you do that."

He stopped to eat a few wild berries.

Thinking of food again, I asked, "What meats do you eat if not fish?"

"Lots of things. Deer, rabbit, horse . . ."

"You don't eat pork or fish, but you'll eat horse?" I must have looked surprised. Sky didn't understand why.

"A horse is clean. A pig is nasty — will eat any-thing. Fish are related to snakes, lizards, and frogs."

"Frog's legs! What could be better?" I said. "And you should taste Mama's fried fish and hush puppies."

"Why eat little puppies? A wood rat is better."

And he wasn't kidding. "You eat rats?" I shouted.

He gave me a real disgusted-like look. "It is a clean animal!"

I said, "You've got mighty peculiar ways."

"So do you."

Chapter 12

In spite of our differences, Sky and I found many more things that we could agree on. We both enjoyed Mama's corn pudding, and his taste for cornbread and molasses was equal to mine.

Although he could speak English very well, Sky needed help understanding words we used like *dang blast it, what-cha-ma-call-it,* and especially some of my made-up words like Un-persons. "I thought you were an Un-person," I told Sky. "Unkind and uncaring. I was wrong. You are *un*possible."

"I do not understand why you would think such a thing of me," he said, smiling devilishly.

It was our love of stories, though, that made it easy for us to share. Nothing made Sky smile quicker than one of my play songs:

Pain in my leg (touch your leg)
Jump, jump!
Pain in my arm (touch your arm)
Jump, jump!
Pain in my head (touch your head)
Jump, jump!
Pain in my neck (touch your neck)
Jump, jump!

One evening when he was mending his boots after it had rained all morning, he told me that Apaches believed the Sun Spirit ran across the sky every day. "After the long rains his moccasin strings were rotten, and he had to stop and fix them. This causes the long days of Large Leaves. By Reddish Brown the strings are replaced and he can move faster and the days are shorter."

I learned a lot about Sky in bits and pieces, for he never talked long or said very much at one time, but what he said was usually worth listening to. His smiles came quicker, and I was beginning to learn that Sky had a good sense of humor. There were many sides to him.

One night, after Papa had read from the Good

73

Book, Sky told us how his father had made him his first bow and arrows and taught him to hunt. "I remember when I was eight or nine, I would run for a long ways with a mouth full of water. I could not swallow it or spit it out. It was like a game, but it was my training to be a warrior." When I tried, I couldn't run from the porch to the road without spitting out the water.

A few nights later, Sky told us that he had ridden on four raids not long before Geronimo surrendered. He wore the raiding cap Geronimo made for him, decorated with feathers of four birds — the oriole, the eagle, the hummingbird, and the quail. Lozen and Naiche, the son of Cochise, and Mangus, the son of Mangas Colorados, were his teachers. "Ordinarily I would have had to wait until I was sixteen to ride on a raid," he explained, "but we had left Fort Apache Reservation and we were on the run. Geronimo allowed me to prove myself at an early age."

"Did you do good?"

"That is not for me to say."

But Mr. Wratten had told us that Sky was considered an adult, so he must have done well. I wanted to know how Sky felt about Mr. Wratten, but I was afraid to mention his name for fear I'd say too much. Papa was going to have to turn Sky in soon or Mr. Wratten was going to come looking for all of us. I was sick at heart about what we were going to do, and lay awake in my loft thinking about it.

Then something happened that changed all of our lives.

Come Friday a week, Papa came running in from the field, calling all of us to the kitchen table, Sky included. He threw off his hat. Beads of sweat formed on his forehead and ran down his cheeks, painting a strange design on his dirty face. His eyes looked like a cornered critter, and his nostrils flared as he sucked in big gulps of air. When I looked at Mama's eyes, I knew something big bad had happened. Crushed in Papa's hand was a cotton leaf. "It's the bo'weevil," he said, pounding his fist against the table. "Lord, Lord, Lord, why have you forsaken me?"

Chapter 13

For the first time in my life I was truly scared — scared that Papa wasn't going to be able to fix what was wrong. The boll weevil was a plague, like one of those God sent Egypt when 'ol Pharaoh wouldn't let God's people go. The Perkins family had lost everything they had when boll weevils ruined their crop. Now they were sharecropping, scattered — some family members in Memphis, some in New Orleans, some in Atlanta — some had gone on out to Iowa, Kansas, and Nebraska. Papa had done all he could to make our farm work. What a shame to be brought low by a tiny bug.

All the time, when Papa was feeling low, Mama talked up and wouldn't let him stay down. And Papa did the same for Mama. Now Papa slumped in his rocker, looking tired and defeated. Mama just clicked her teeth and shook her head, saying, "Umph, umph, umph." I had never seen both of them so soul sick at the same time.

Sky sat beside me, trying to get a grasp of what we were so worried about. He'd never heard of a boll weevil. I did my best to explain it, but my words came out jumbled and confused the way they did when I was excited.

After a while, Sky stood up. At first, I thought he was going to leave, but he politely asked if he might speak. Papa gave him permission.

"For all things there is a beginning," Sky began, speaking slowly, almost unsure about continuing. Papa encouraged him to go on. "For all things there is an end. Then there is a new beginning. There will be no harvest this year. That is an end. Tomorrow starts your new beginning. What will it be?" Sky sat back down.

Papa nodded his approval. "That's mighty fine thinking," he said. "Your Papa teach you that?"

"I grow up with those words. They are a part of what we believe."

Papa picked up his Bible as he usually did during

trouble. "There's a like idea in this book," he said. "Says there's a time for everything — a time to live and a time to die; a time to plant and a time to harvest, and so on — a time for everything."

It all sounded like talk to me — feel-good words. But no high-sounding ideas could kill the boll weevils. No pretty passages could pay off Papa's debt.

"What are we going to do?" I begged to know.

"Jane," Papa said, shaking his head. "Looks like we might have to give up. Lord might be telling us it's time to . . ."

"No!" I wouldn't let him finish. "Don't say that. We can't give up our home."

"That's enough, Sarah. We might have to," Mama put in.

"You taught me to be proud and to hold on to my dreams," I said, refusing to back down. "How can you give up so easily?"

"I think you've said enough," said Mama, her eyes flashing anger.

I climbed up the ladder to my loft, fell across my bed, and wept bitterly. Where was Mama's hope? Where was Papa's faith? Mean trouble was hanging over us like a funeral shroud, even in my loft where I always felt safe and free.

Lying awake, a small thought began to nag at me. I kept feeling like there was something I should remember, something ... but what? I thought and thought, then at last, it came to me. "Please let it be there," I said, wishing, hoping, and praying. Sure enough, the handbill that Lath Jones had passed out about Tuskegee was still tucked away in the pocket of my Sunday dress. In it was a notice from Booker T. Washington asking for carpenters to build desks. Papa was a fine carpenter. Why couldn't he build the desks Mr. Washington needed?

"Papa," I shouted, forgetting that it was in the middle of the night. But he answered me just the same. I showed him the note: "This is a way to beat the boll weevil." He read the notice:

Attention all colored carpenters.
Use your talent to build school desks
and tables, earn money, be independent.

"Bless be ... maybe ... just maybe ...," he whispered, daring to hope again. "I'll go see Lath Jones first thing in the morning."

Papa greeted daylight fully dressed and ready to go. Grabbing his hat, he headed out the door. "Come on," Papa said. "You, too, Sky." Buster didn't need an invitation. He just came along.

We followed Papa down the road, through the woods, past Payne Chapel A.M.E. Church, and another mile to Lath Jones's house. Although he had a wife and two children, they were making a great sacrifice for him to attend Tuskegee. His plans were to maybe become a teacher and start a school here in Quincy. Miz Annie, his wife, took in laundry to help support her husband's schooling. A whole lot of us wanted Lath Jones to be successful.

Miz Annie was already in the yard washing up when we came. "Morning," she said. "Ya'l up mighty early." Papa introduced Miz Annie to Sky. She eyed the boy curiously. "Word tell that you and Georgianne had an Indian living on yo' place. How'd ya'l come by him?"

"He's an Apache. Reckon he found us," said Papa. "Been sick, though. Georgianne and Jane brought him back by help of the good Lord, I reckon."

"Fine-looking boy, he is," she said, calling over her shoulder. "Lath. Company here." Then turning to

Papa she whispered, "Had trouble last night. Big trouble."

So we weren't the only ones having trouble, I thought.

Mr. Janes came to the door. His face was brusied and his arm was in a sling.

"What happened?" Papa asked, shock darkening his eyes.

"Had a visit from the Knights of the Southern Order of Manhood last evening," Mr. Jones said, anger still trembling his voice. He offered Papa a seat, and Sky and I sat on the steps. Buster lay at our feet, for the moment.

"I memorized the Constitution word for word, just as they say to pass the literacy test," Mr. Jones said. "When I did it, then they come up with I needed to know all the amendments, too."

"You don't mean it?" Papa asked in disbelief. "Times are changing fast. If we don't do something, we're gon' be right back in slavery."

"I plan to vote come November and I will not be turned around by all the tricks they can think up," he said. I wanted to believe that Lath Jones would not — could not be stopped. But so many people had been.

"Did you report this attack to Sheriff Johnson?" Papa asked.

Mr. Jones shrugged. "What good would it do? No white man is going to take up our side against their own, least 'til they need our votes. Then they show up making all kind of promises."

Papa nodded, but still encouraged Mr. Jones to make a report. "Trouble is we need our own people running for sheriff and the city council. We got as much sense as some of the whites that's running."

"You make a good point," said Lath. I liked the idea, too.

Miz Annie stood up from over the washtub. "Lee Andy," she said sternly. "Don't go encouraging Lath to get into no mo' trouble than he's in. If you think them Knights gon' sit still while we vote colored people into offices they reckon belongs to them, then you both crazier than you sound. Now I know you didn't come all the way over here this early in the morning to get my day started off wrong."

Papa couldn't help but agree that Miz Annie had every reason to be scared. But I agreed with Papa. We needed to do something to stop the Knights. And if that meant running people for office who could fight them, then that's what we needed to do. I thought Mr. Jones would make a great leader. But, I doubted that Miz Annie would ever let him. The Knights had scared all the fight out of her.

That's when Papa told Mr. Jones about the boll weevil getting his cotton. Then he explained how he planned to save his farm by maybe making desks for Mr. Booker T. Washington's school up in Tuskegee.

"It's true that Mr. Booker T. Washington needs desks for his students," said Mr. Jones, "and he's willing to pay a master carpenter a fine fee for making them."

"I got a woods full of cedar, pine, oak, and walnut trees. I got my daddy's tools, and I'm a good carpenter. There are plenty of men around here that need work. They can help me."

Mr. Jones smiled broadly. "That's exactly what Professor Washington wants us to do, be industrious. But you know if you take this on, you'll be targeted by the Knights."

"We're not afraid of them," I said. Sky nodded his approval.

Mr. Jones laughed outright. "Well, well," he said to Papa. "You have quite an army here." Then looking at us very seriously he added, "You'll need one."

"I got no choice," said Papa.

"Well," said Mr. Jones, "I'll write Mr. Washington about you today. He has accepted our invitation to speak at the Founder's Day program in a few weeks. That would be a great time for you to meet him, and maybe show him a sample of your work."

Papa's spirits were lifted. When we got home, Sky went to check on Big Two, while Papa and I told Mama about our visit.

"I know I can make a fine desk," said Papa, filled with confidence.

To my surprise, Mama didn't support him the way I thought she would. "Poor Lath. Poor Annie," she said, kneading bread. "It's a wonder those Knights didn't hurt him worse. They hung a man over in Bakersfield last month. Maybe we should just get out from down here in Alabama," she said. "Go north like all the others." She turned the bread dough over and over in her hands, slapping it, poking it, slamming it down on the table.

"But buildin' the desks is a way that will 'llow us to keep our land, build a future for ourselves and Jane," Papa said, almost pleading.

"No," insisted Mama. "We need to leave here, now," she said, pushing the heels of her hands into the dough.

Papa seemed to waver. He fingered the fringe on the bottom of Mama's curtains. "I know you're upset. But, Georgianne, we just can't walk away from everything we've got!"

"What we got, Lee Andy?" Mama shouted, wiping her hands on her apron. "This little piece of dirt? This house? Is it worth working yo'self to death for? Is it worth dying for? Work night and day for a storm or a bug to take it all 'way. Raise your head up to look at the sun, and here comes the Knights to stomp you back down into the dirt! I'm ready to go!" Mama didn't mean that, I told myself. But when I looked in her eyes, I knew that she did. "When you add it all up, we aine got nothing!"

Sky came in the door at the same time Papa was fleeing to the barn. Oh, no, I thought. Mama had won again. She was like Miz Annie, so scared of what might happen she couldn't think straight. But nobody ever fought the Knights and people like them; they'd just keep on. But Papa was back in minutes. "I can't go along with you, Georgianne," he said strongly. "You're wrong. We do have something here. And I aim to take a stand, to hold on to what's ours. Now you can be with me on this or a'gin me."

Sky stood by Papa. My heart sank. Sky was willing to stand with us, and we were going to send him back to his captors. I took a deep breath and went and stood on the other side of Papa.

Mama turned away, covering her face as she wept. "I don't know what got into me," she said. "I'm so ashamed for discouraging you. I'm just so scared."

"It's a foolish person who don't get scared when it's time to be so," Papa used one of his favorite sayings. "But we're gon' be all right by and by."

"I'm with you, Papa," I said, unable to still my tongue.

Sky sent up a whoop that rattled the pots on the wall. "I had planned to leave on this day," he said. "But now I will not. I will stand with you, Lee Andy, *shik'ise,* my brother."

"You ought to know something, before you decide to stay," Papa said. "I was going to town today to wire Mr. Wratten to come get you. But if you want to stay with us, I'm gon' do whatever I can to make sure you stay right here as long as you want to."

This was the way our "new beginning" started. I felt relieved that everything was out in the open. Sky wasn't going to leave us and we weren't going to break his trust and turn him in.

Papa wrote a long letter to Mr. Wratten spelling out our situation and telling how attached we had become to Sky. Then he explained about the boll weevil, and asked if Sky could remain with us as an apprentice, hired to help with a furniture-making business he was starting. The letter sounded very impressive when I read it aloud.

"I think you'd stay just to eat Mama's fried green tomatoes," I said, teasing Sky.

CHAPTER 14

Over the next few weeks, Papa spent every waking minute working on a desk design. Something that was sturdy but easy to build. I stood watching over Papa's shoulder as he drew lines on paper, then scratched them out, only to start over again. At last, he came up with an idea for a chair and desk that were all in one.

Then it was time to build the model.

Papa had some lumber in the barn he'd been saving to make me a bigger chest, but now he used it to build his model desk. I didn't care. I'd get a chest later.

During the weeks that followed, Papa and Sky developed a fast friendship and I developed a very bad feeling toward Sky. He and Papa stayed huddled up in the barn, working for hours. I only got to see them at meals. "He has the makings of a master craftsman,"

Papa bragged. "His hands move over the wood with an understanding."

And even when they weren't working they did things together — the things Papa used to do with me.

"Come on, let's go," Papa said one evening, taking Sadie off the wall, I was almost out the door before I realized he was talking to Sky. *I* had always hunted with Papa!

While they were gone, I sat brooding on the porch, conjuring up bad ideas. So when they came back dragging a deer and toting a wild turkey, I didn't say a word. They didn't seem to notice me and went right on swapping stories, laughing and joking. "You ought to see Sky use that bow and arrow," he said. "He can hit a flea on a rabbit's ear at fifty paces. You've got to teach me how to use one of them things," Papa said, studying the bow and arrow.

I didn't like the little mean thoughts that were taking shape in my mind, but I couldn't make them go away either. With each passing day I grew more and more resentful of the time Papa spent with Sky.

Then my jealousy spread to Mama.

One morning after gathering eggs and milking January, I found Sky busy building something in the yard. So far, it had four posts with a roof made of branches. "The Mexicans call it a ramada, Little Bush. I made it for Miss Georgianne."

"Don't call me Little Bush," I snapped at him. "My name is Sarah Jane." I walked away in a huff.

When Sky presented the ramada to Mama, the biggest grin spread across her face. I couldn't believe how much she was making over that old lean-to. "This takes me back," she said, remembering. "Grandma Jen used to work outside all the time — out where she could get fresh air, but still be protected from the sun."

She patted Sky on the arm. "What did we do 'fore you came?" she said. "You've brought so much joy to us all." Then she turned to me, asking, "Isn't that right, Sarah?"

I just walked away, heading for the garden where I could feed my jealousy with more mean thoughts. When I heard Buster barking in the barn, I called to my friend, but he didn't come. So I went to find him. He was sitting beside Sky, his tail flapping from side to side. "Come, Buster!" He looked to me and then to Sky.

"Go on," said Sky. And Buster obeyed *his* command.

All the ugliness that had overcome my spirit rumbled out of me like a foul wind and I took it out on Buster. "You're a stupid, stupid dog!"

Buster may not have understood my words, but he felt the anger in them. He tucked his tail between his legs, his ears drooped and, to add to my frustration, he went and stood beside Sky like the well-behaved dog we all knew he wasn't.

Sky recognized the meaning of every hateful word I'd said, but even if I'd wanted to I couldn't stop the rush of angry words that came out of me. "Why don't you just run away?" I shouted. "I don't want you to stay. Why don't you run — run somewhere!"

CHAPTER 15

"An only child sometimes has a tiny heart," Sky said before leaving me in the barn to wallow in my own puddle of meanness.

I spent the day moping and trying to warm up to Buster. He avoided me, and I avoided Sky. "I'm sorry" is a lot easier to feel than it is to say — especially for an Un-person like me. I had become an unkind, unfriendly, unhappy person — my own worst enemy.

Sky carried on as if nothing had happened. He busied himself building something made of bent poles and branches. I knew what it was because he had described it to me. It was an Apache house. Women usually built them, but being out on his own Sky was building one for himself. He told me some people called them *wickiups,* but the Apaches just called them houses. Since he enjoyed sleeping outside, that's probably where he was going to sleep. I tried not to care.

Papa got home late that evening, bringing news from town. I was in the loft, looking out at them as Mama showed off the ramada Sky had made. Then he invited my folks to sleep outside in the wickiup he had built. One look at it and Papa declared: "I aine 'bout to sleep in that."

"What harm will it do?" said Mama. "There is nothing more wonderful than sleeping under a blanket of stars. I'd like to try it."

Papa must have visited the barn three times before he'd convinced himself that sleeping under God's heavens was worth trying. "Just for this one night," he said. "But this aine gon' be no regular thing."

"Anything you say," said Mama.

Lying on my bed I felt lonely and left out, and my loft was close and stuffy. Nobody had asked where I was or why I wasn't with them. I eased to the window and listened for a while. Their laughter seemed to draw me down the stairs. Standing in the shadows where I could see but not be seen, I ached to be near them.

Papa was describing how when he was a boy he and a friend had stolen a chicken and cooked it without cleaning its insides out. He laughed so, his whole body shook. I had heard that story a hundred times, but his voice sounded so different — light, younger somehow. All the worry of the past few weeks seemed to have melted away.

Sky told about when he had been an Un-person. He used my word in his story. I listened closely. "I was unkind to my good friend. I was jealous because his mother had made my friend a beautiful shirt to wear to a dance. I ripped up my friend's shirt and buried it," he said. "All my relatives knew what I had done. And they treated me as if I were invisible. They asked, 'Where is Sky?' I said, 'Here I am,' but they acted like they didn't see me. Then when I gave my cousin my own shirt, my mother shouted with happiness, 'Here is my good son.'"

By then, I had come out on the front porch and was sitting on the steps. Buster came and licked my hand. He had forgiven me. Would Sky? I wondered. "Can Little Bush come out and be with you?" I asked.

"The home is the heart of every family," said Sky. "It is large enough to include all those who want to be inside it. Come, *shilahe,* my sister, and sit with us."

Sky was my brother and I loved him. Now I knew what Edna Mae meant when she said her brothers were awful. They really were when she was mad at them, but that had nothing to do with her *real* feelings — the feelings of the heart. "I'm sorry, Sky. You are really *shilahe*."

Although Mama and Papa didn't know the whole story, they suspected it had something to do with me being jealous of the attention they showed Sky.

"We are fortunate to have a loving and caring daughter," said Mama.

Papa pulled my braids affectionately and gave me a peppermint stick. "Bought this for the smartest girl in Alabama." I broke it in half and gave a piece to Sky. He'd never had peppermint before. I was sure it wasn't going to be the last.

For a long while I lay still, listening to the crickets chirping and the flip-flop flip-flop of Buster's tail as he lay contented between us. A train whistle blew in the distance, and I didn't wish to be on it — not just then. Papa always said that the only thing perfect was God. If that was so, then that night was God-sent.

Chapter 16

Sky respected Papa in all ways, but there were two things Papa could not get Sky to do — go fishing and go to church. Whenever Papa brought out his Bible, Sky found something else to do elsewhere. I knew why he wouldn't fish, but I didn't know why he would not go to church. As far as I could tell, Sky was a very spiritual person, who was more Christian in his ways than some folks who claimed to be.

One night while I was finishing the dishes, I overheard Mama and Papa talking about Sky's religion.

"If I could get him to go to church, learn the Bible," said Papa. "I wish I could get him to see . . ."

Mama never stopped snapping beans. "I say we leave Sky alone. He's got his own beliefs and we should respect them, same as he does ours. You don't see him trying to make us study on his god, Ysun."

"But we are supposed to go out and try to bring in other souls to the faith," Papa argued.

"Did you ever consider that Jesus never beat anybody into the church, but he beat wrong-minded people out of it?"

Papa took offense. "Now, what's that supposed to mean, Georgianne?"

"You decide."

Mama was right, I thought. Sky had his own way of looking at the world. If we tried to change him, then we were as bad as that school he didn't want to go to.

CHAPTER 17

Papa didn't celebrate the Fouth of July holiday, stayed away from town, and wouldn't be in the parade. "We colored people aine got nothing to celebrate about," he said to the congregation after Sunday service. "When the Knights stop riding; when our barns stop being burned; when our livestock stops being killed, then we'll have something to celebrate." Not a black person showed up in Quincy on the Fourth. Papa treated it like it was any other workday, and plowed over the ruined cotton plants that the boll weevils had destroyed.

Sheriff Ray Johnson came riding out to the farm a few evenings later. "Missed y'all in town at the big celebration," he said, standing in the yard waiting for Mama to invite him to sit down. She didn't and left him standing there shifting from foot to foot. At last, Papa stepped down off the porch and talked to him in the yard.

"I'll get straight to the point," said the sheriff. "Word is out you been hit by the boll weevils. That don't look good for you, now does it?"

"I reckon not," Papa answered.

"Well, I just want you to know that I'm not agin' you, Lee Andy. Shoot, we been knowing each other since we was boys. That's why I'm gon' give you a deal. See, I'm willing to forgive the debt if you'll sign over the farm to me and stay on and sharecrop. I'll split with you 70–30."

Mama leaped to her feet. Papa held up his hand the way he did when he wasn't finished talking yet. "Sheriff Johnson," he said calmly. "I 'preciate your offer, but I've got other plans."

The sheriff looked surprised. Then he chuckled. It was a soft wicked sound. "And what kind of plan do you have, Lee Andy?"

"Well," said Papa, returning to the porch. "I haven't quite worked it out in my head yet, but one thing I know, it don't include sharecropping. But not to worry, you'll get paid all that I owe you."

The sheriff mounted his horse. "Don't 'pear to me like you got a choice. Better think on my offer 'fore it's too late. Somebody else might not be as fair as I'm trying to me." And he rode away.

"Get thee behind me, Satan," Papa whispered just loud enough for me to hear.

"Fair!" Mama shouted. "Did you hear him talkin' 'bout fair?" She was purely put out. "He really thinks it's fair for you to work yo'self to death," she said to Papa, adding, "just so he can take seventy cents out of every dollar you make?" Papa didn't need to say anything. He had already made himself clear.

But I couldn't help but think Mama had been right to not trust Sheriff Johnson. There was something about him that didn't seem real. His lips turned up in a broad smile, but his small, dark eyes were cold and without feeling. They weren't human eyes. No, Mama was right. Sheriff Johnson wasn't to be trusted.

Soon after, the heat really set in. Days folded into days, each one equally as hot as the one before. There was no sign of relief, not a cloud in the sky, and the hot-hot days of late August were yet to come. On one of those endless chains of muggy, miserable days,

Buster told us somebody was coming long before he got there.

Reverend Henry, the pastor of Payne Chapel A.M.E. Church, came around the side of the house, puffing and blowing and panting. Buster was barking and playfully nipping at his heels. Reverend Henry flopped in one of the porch chairs and caught his breath. "I see that dog of yours is as untrained as ever."

"He let us know you were comin'," said Mama, chuckling. Reverend Henry reminded me of a rooster who thought the sun rose because he crowed, but he was nice enough. At least his smile looked real.

Wiping his face with a large white handkerchief, Reverend Henry announced in his preachery voice that Mr. Washington would be at the church come Sunday, and he wanted to make sure there was a good turnout. "And there is going to be a basket supper after morning service. I do hope you make one of your custard pies, Miz Georgianne."

Sky came from the barn with a piece of wood. "Mr. Lee Andy, is this the way you want the desk leg rounded?"

"Perfect," said Papa. He then introduced Sky to Reverend Henry and told him how much Sky had helped him get the desk model made. "Heard you had an Indian living here." Sky excused himself. "Fine young man, I'm sure," Reverend Henry said, waiting until Sky was out of hearing range. He sent me to get a glass of water at the well, but I still heard him say, "If that boy cuts his hair and puts on a suit of clothes, he'll fit right in. And please make him take that earring out of his ear."

Mama started to say something, but Papa put in quickly, "Well, Reverend Henry, I reckon King David wore an earring," he said. "And besides, Sky is a natural-born Chiricahua Apache. I reckon he's sure to stay one." Mama gave that quick victorious nod of her head and disappeared into the kitchen where she let out a big whoop!

Reverend Henry didn't know what to think, so he suddenly remembered that he had business at the church and left in a hurry.

CHAPTER 18

Sunday started with the promise of being a nice day, but by church time, the wind had picked up and it looked like we were in for an Alabama thunderstorm. We needed the relief, though, so none of us was sad.

Mama picked a few pieces of lint off Papa's Sunday vest and straightened his hat. She checked Sky and smiled approvingly. He did look especially handsome in his white shirt and new vest Mama had made him out of cowhide. He was only coming along with us to help with the desk. "You aine got to go in," Papa had promised. "You can stay right outside and talk to Ysun if you want. I reckon God, Ysun, Jehovah, they all the same anyway."

Mama had also made crowns of fresh wildflowers that she placed on my head and on hers. Then dabbing a spot of vanilla behind each ear, she said, "There. We will smell as good as we look."

Papa allowed that we should be more modest, but he didn't think a thing of boasting about the desk, even though it was special — something to be real proud of. "I wouldn't mind sitting in one of those desks," I said.

"Maybe one day you will."

I thought about that all the way to church. Me sitting in a school desk of my own, reading from a book, and writing on real paper. Nothing in the world could be better than that, 'cept'n maybe riding a train.

Sky had never been anywhere public with us before, so he caused quite a stir at church. Word was out and around that an Indian was living with us, but most folks figured he was a Seminole or a Creek. "This is Sky and he is a Chiricahua Apache," I said, showing him off. I could tell he was embarassed with all the fuss being made over him. But I was mighty proud of my brother, the way he walked with his shoulders back, his head high, and his eyes straight ahead.

"Look at them," I whispered softly. "You're the envy of every boy, and all the girls are making eyes at you." Anybody else would have been flattered. But not Sky. All the attention, even the curious looks and silly chatter, never seemed to touch him — not inside, where it mattered most.

Papa asked Sky to see after the desk, and that's what he did, taking his place beside the wagon. Meanwhile I went to visit my friends. It was good seeing everybody, especially Edna Mae. She was living in Quincy, housekeeping for a family, and only got to come home once a month. Edna Mae didn't look very happy, but she never said exactly why and I didn't ask. Several white ladies had asked Mama about hiring me out, but Mama always said no. And Papa would have none of it either. The whole thing reminded him too much of the way slave girls were sold away with no regard for their mother's or father's wishes. Even when I'd offered to hire out to help after the crop failed, Papa would have none of it.

Leola Prime was back home after visiting her grandmother in Atlanta. She was sporting a new dress and being real uppity. Avery Napier pulled my braids and ran but Mother Gray caught him by the ear and made him help her up the steps of the church. We kids thought Mother Gray had been there when God said, "Let there be light," and she'd still be around when

Gabriel blew the trumpet on Judgment Day. Nobody wanted to be on the bad side of Mother Gray. So I waited until her back was turned and poked my tongue out at Avery.

About that time, the undertaker, Brother Pauly Crossman — not kin to us by blood, but by plantation — arrived with Mr. Booker T. Washington. They came up in a fine horse-drawn carriage, the kind Papa said his old master used to have. Not too many people could afford a horse like that — white or black. Still, it made everybody feel real good knowing that their last ride would be in something pulled by a horse that grand.

The clouds hung heavy overhead. Everybody hurried to greet Mr. Washington. He was an impressive-looking man, tall, with kind eyes and an honest smile. It didn't take much to see why he was so well-liked. He had such an easy way of talking, people felt comfortable being around him.

Thunder rumbled in the distance and a raindrop fell on my nose. As we all quickly filed inside the church, Reverend Henry and Mr. Washington leading the way, I looked over my shoulder to see where Sky was. He was standing by the wagon, watching over the desk and paying no attention to the weather. I beckoned for him to come inside, but he shook his head. "Leave him be," Mama whispered.

As usual, Reverend Henry chanted the call to worship. Mr. Thompson said a prayer and the congregation sang all six verses of "God Delivered Daniel." Then Reverend Henry spent twenty minutes introducing Mr. Washington, praising him for all his accomplishments. Women were fanning, men tugged at their collars, and we children were getting fidgety. But when Mr. Washington began to speak, everybody settled down.

"I am pleased you invited me here today. My message is a simple one and it won't take long to deliver it," he said, speaking to the congregation. "We have come through some stormy times and we are going to experience more difficult times." Amens spread throughout the church. "I believe we must learn how to build and grow and take care of ourselves," he continued, "learn to make the shirts we wear on our back, fix our own machinery, lay brick, build buildings, and make furniture in such a way that we earn the respect of those who would condemn us as inferiors. I am not saying we should not continue to struggle for justice, but we need to move more slowly, let the idea of equality become more acceptable to those in power."

Papa said a resounding amen, but Mama didn't. I listened more closely to what Mr. Washington was saying. He went on about how colored people only upset whites when they pushed to be equal. "We need to better ourselves, and be more patient. Stop complaining about rights."

Papa said amen again. Mama leaned back and folded her arms and sat stony still. "To my way of thinking, we already equal," she mumbled under her breath. I said amen to that.

I didn't hear much more of what Mr. Washington had to say, because I was trying to make sense out of what he'd already said. While I disagreed with most of his words, there were a few things that made sense. That's what was so confusing. What good did it do to work hard and build a business and the Knights came and burned it down? I decided Mr. Washington didn't know too much about what was going on in southern Alabama. Maybe up in Tuskegee things were different. If he knew, then maybe Mr. Washington would change his talk about not fighting about rights.

After service, we were happy to see that the storm had passed over without a heavy rain. Mama and I joined other women who set up for the basket supper.

"Well, what did you think?" Papa asked Mama. I could tell he was nervous and full of excitement. "Smart man, aine he?"

Mama grunted. "You think so?" She busied herself arranging fresh-baked pies on a quilt and placing fresh fruit and flowers in between. Mama could make the simplest things look so pretty. But Papa could tell she wasn't prettying up her opinion of Mr. Washington.

"Don't start, Georgianne," Papa whispered, looking over his shoulders as Mr. Lath Jones and Mr. Washington came toward us. "Keep yo' mouth and you, too, Jane."

Me? I couldn't believe Papa would think I'd say something out of the way to Mr. Washington. We all knew how important making those desks was to Papa. If there was a possible chance to save our farm, it would be with Mr. Washington's help. Mama and I may not have agreed with all Mr. Washington had to say, but we weren't going to spoil it for Papa.

Mr. Lath Jones came up all happy, introducing Mr. Washington to us. Mama smiled real pleasant-like. "Won't you have a slice of pie?" she asked graciously. Mama could be a charmer when she wanted to be. I could see Papa breathe a little easier.

"Lath tells me you and your father built all the pews in the church and the pit as well. Impressive work."

Papa modestly accepted the compliment, showing Mr. Washington to the wagon where Sky was waiting with the desk. He threw off the cloth. There were oohs and aahs all around. Everybody had to agree, it was a right smart piece of carpentry. I sure was proud of it, and stuck out my chest.

"This is fine, fine workmanship," said Mr. Washington, rubbing his hands over the smooth finish. "I always say the mark of a good craftsman is in the details. I like this all-in-one design very much. What is this?" He pointed to a cluster of leaves carved in the back of the chair.

"A yucca plant that grows in the Southwest Territory where Sky lived." Papa pulled Sky to his side and introduced him as his apprentice. "He's quite an artist."

Mr. Washington shook hands with Sky and smiled warmly. "The details make this desk like no others I've seen. When you have learned all you can from this man, think about coming to Tuskegee. There is a place for you there."

Sky acknowledged Mr. Washington's offer with a courteous nod.

"This is my daughter, Sarah Jane," Papa said, pulling me in front of him. "She's the one who gave me the idea to build the desks. She's real smart." Papa had never said that about me before. The words covered me like one of Mama's quilts, and I felt my face tingle warmly.

"Are girls welcomed at Tuskegee?" I asked.

"They most certainly are," said Mr. Washington. We have students from all over the country attending Tuskegee — male, female, Japanese, and Chinese, and Indians. I hope you'll come join us one day soon."

Then, turning to Papa, Mr. Washington extended his hand. "I think you are a fine example of the kind of craftsman the colored race needs more of. Come let's talk about the details."

When they went off to discuss business more

privately, Sky took Mama and me aside. "We are being watched," he said. "There are five men on horseback watching us from the woods."

"The Knights," Mama said, gasping.

"Maybe," he answered, hardly above a whisper.

As hard as I tried, I couldn't see with Sky's eyes. He always said I couldn't see because my mind was always racing around from idea to idea. So, I calmed myself and tried to empty all the thinking out of my head. Then I looked into the trees, searching, looking, looking. There! A rider standing in the shadow of a tree. "I see one," I whispered. "What do you think they will do?"

"Nothing, for now."

"They're just checking up on us," Mama put in. "Don't trouble Lee Andy with this right now. This is his hour. Let him enjoy it for just a little while."

Sky nodded his agreement, but I could see he was ever watchful, ready to spring into action if necessary.

After what seemed an hour or longer, the meeting ended. Papa climbed to the back of his wagon and called for everybody's attention. "Listen close," he said. "Professor Washington has offered me a contract to make forty desks by the next school term come

October." People cheered and applauded. Papa went on, his voice sounding brave and commanding. "I've got a woods full of timber, and Mr. Washington says he'll send equipment to plane it, and even now give me a down payment so as to get started. Now all I need is some good, reliable help. I can't pay you much, but I can pay a whole lot more than sharecropping. Who will work with me on this?" Papa was real fired up. "If we can get this off the ground it could mean regular work for all of us."

People began discussing the offer with one another. Some heads were nodding and others weren't. Mama closed her eyes and crossed her fingers. Even though Papa said such things didn't work, I did it, too, and whispered a prayer.

"Don't be afraid to help your neighbor," said Mr. Washington. "We must show that we can do business with one another before we can ask others to do business with us."

"It beats sharecropping," said Mr. Thompson, jumping up on the wagon next to Papa. "Me and my four boys is with you, Lee Andy."

"Count me in," said another man.

"Me, too," put in another.

113

Cheers went up all around. Cheers for Mr. Washington. Cheers for Papa, who pulled Mama and me up on the wagon next to him. We were all laughing and crying at the same time. Papa called for Sky to join us, which he did. But I noticed that he never took his eyes off the woods.

CHAPTER 19

True to his word, in a few weeks Mr. Washington sent an advance of money and shipped all the equipment Papa needed to mill and plane the lumber for the desks. Mr. Thompson helped Papa round up men with wagons to meet him at the train depot to haul it all back to the farm.

"People been mighty curious 'bout what we doing," said Lath Jones. "I told them we were trying to better ourselves by doing for ourselves," he said.

"Tol' 'em right," Papa said. In her own way, Mama had warned him about the Knights watching us at the church. So we were all half expecting for them to try something. Now that the equipment had come from Tuskegee, we were sure they were going to strike. We just didn't know when.

That's why Mama was beside herself when Papa agreed to stand with Lath Jones when he took the literacy test. Mr. Jones had memorized the complete constitution and all fifteen of the amendments just so he could vote. "You don't need to stir up no hornet's nest," Mama had argued. But nothing could stop Papa from helping a friend, no matter what the consequences were.

"I gave my word, and that's my bond." Then, assuring Mama, he added, "We shouldn't be forced to live in fear all our natural born days."

Papa sent the wagons on ahead, and he and Mr. Jones headed toward the courthouse. He promised to meet Sky and me in an hour at Centennial Square.

There wasn't an hour's worth of anything to do in Quincy. The town was built around the square, and nothing had changed much since old slavery days. On the north side was the train station where I loved to watch passengers coming and going. Once one of the porters had let me sit in a sleeping-car coach. The seats let down into beds. I closed my eyes and thought of riding on that train to far, far away places.

Next to the station was the Quincy Hotel. When colored people went in they were told there were no rooms. A white person could come in right behind a black one and get a room. Colored weren't welcome. The courthouse where Papa voted and paid his taxes was located on the east side of the square. There was a time when slaves were sold on the courthouse steps. On the north side was the general store, a barber shop, and a newspaper office. The Peppermill Theater was located on the south side — an ugly pink building with no windows on the front. Posted on the door was a sign that said, "No colored allowed." Signs like that were going up all over town.

In the middle of the square was a bandstand where candidates made speeches on the Fourth of July. "This is Quincy," I told Sky. "The place where I was born. Aine much — just a little dinky Alabama town."

"It is your spot," he said softly, stopping in front of a statue. I hardly ever noticed it being there anymore.

"That's President Andrew Jackson," I said. "He's a hero to folks 'round here, but Mama's got no use for him 'cause of the way he did the Seminoles and all the other Indians who lived east of the Mississippi."

We strolled to the bandstand and sat on the steps. A blue jay fussed at a squirrel that had gotten too close to her nest. "On the other hand," I went on, "Papa said

Andrew Jackson freed all the black slaves who fought with him during the Battle of New Orleans. They called themselves Free Jacks. Truth is, I don't know what to think of Jackson."

The squirrel scampered to another tree to get away from the angry mama jay. Sky shook his head. "Jackson is like many of the *'Indaa* that invaded our homeland — confusing. On the reservation we saw all kinds of white men — some bad, some worse."

"Then there are those like Mr. Wratten. He's not bad, is he?"

"No," said Sky. "He does what he can. That is better than most. He has the Chiricahua at heart, and we think of him as a brother. He came here with us and for this his father will have nothing more to do with him."

I couldn't imagine me doing anything that would displease Papa and Mama that much. Sky studied the statue for a moment or two more.

Just about that time we saw Mr. Jones come running out of the courthouse. He leaped on his horse and let out a shout for joy as he rode away. "He must have passed the literacy test," I said. Minutes later,

Papa and Sheriff Johnson came out of the door and stood on the courthouse steps to talk. Papa was smiling, so I figured everything was going all right.

Papa could talk for an hour without coming up for breath. And since it was hot and due to get hotter, I decided to take Sky over to Tucker's General Store and get a lemonade. That proved to be a big mistake.

First thing I saw when I walked in the door was a big sign saying that the state of Alabama had passed a law forbidding blacks to buy firearms, certain calibers of bullets, and no blasting powder.

"How will people hunt?" I asked.

Mr. Tucker didn't answer just then. He never took his eyes off Sky. The idea of Sky moving around the store, looking at all the things that were on display — cloth, thread, foods, all kinds of tools — seemed to make Mr. Tucker uneasy. "How should I know how Lee Andy will hunt?" he said. "Use a bow and arrow, I 'spose." Then he laughed nervously, looking at Sky like he was sour. "What kind of something is he? He aine Creek or Seminole, but he's an Indian, aine he? Where you from, boy?"

Sky answered in Apache. That didn't set well with

Mr. Tucker. "Speak American, boy?" Sky spoke again in Apache. From what he'd been teaching me, I could figure out he had called Mr. Tucker a fool.

I could feel trouble tingling in my toes. I had to get Sky out of there. Just as we pushed through the door, we bumped into the Farley brothers, who were coming in.

They were two of the meanest Un-persons who ever stepped into a pair of britches. They were un-everything! I was convinced they'd been nursed at birth by a rattlesnake. Buck was the oldest, a large burly man, natural-born mean. He'd lost an arm during the Civil War, and that made him meaner.

With the body of a man and the sense of a gnat, his brother, Jack, was just as ornery. His simple minded grin seemed more funny than threatening, but when Jack stopped grinning, trouble usually started. The Farley brothers hated everybody, but they had a special pick against all colored people.

Their father had been a foreman at The Pines, but he'd been fired by the Crossman family. Word tell he'd whipped a slave to death because the man had stopped to get a drink of water without getting Farley's permission. The other slaveholders wouldn't hire him because the goal was not to kill slaves, which was like throwing away good money, but to keep them working. Ol' man Farley passed his hatred on to his boys.

It was too late to warn Sky about any of this.

Jack looked at Sky with disbelieving eyes. "Well, I swear," he said, grinning stupidly. "Did you ever see such purty hair. It's hanging down past his shoulders. Looks like a woman's hair — aine right on a man." Jack reached out to touch Sky's hair, but Sky moved away with such speed it threw Jack off balance.

"I know what you is," hissed Buck. "I seen yo' kind over in Pensacola. You're one of them murdering Apaches. Let's have some fun, Jack." I had seen how the Farleys had fun. One of the Thompson boys would walk with a limp all his days because the Farley brothers were having fun.

The fire in Sky's eyes flamed up. I didn't think he had a chance against the two Farleys. Even though Buck didn't have but one arm, Sky was still out-numbered and out-sized. He beckoned for me to move away. I stepped behind him, all the time looking for something I could hit one of the Farleys with if he got the best of Sky.

"Man shouldn't have hair that long," Buck said, sliding a knife from his boot. Mr. Tucker shook his head and laughed.

Jack giggled, a sick high-pitched sound. "No earring neither." Then he stopped grinning.

"Watch out, Sky," I hollered, but it was too late. Jack sprang at Sky, grabbing him around the neck. Buck moved in, aiming to cut off Sky's hair and heaven knows what else. But Sky reared up and kicked Buck in the chest, and Buck went sprawling to the ground. In one quick move, Sky twisted his body around, breaking Jack's hold, and sent him crashing down on top of his brother.

Sky always seemed so quiet and so gentle, hardly ever speaking above a whisper. But seeing him in action reminded me of what Mr. Wratten had said. Sky could take care of himself. I stopped worrying and stood back to enjoy seeing the Farley brothers get their due. Mr. Tucker took out running toward the sheriff's office — to get help, I supposed.

Picking up the knife, Sky leaped on Buck's back and grabbed his head, yanking it back to expose his throat. Jack made a move toward them, but stopped short when he saw Sky place the sharp blade against his brother's forehead. "You should not be so snippity," Sky said. Sky looked at me and winked. "What if I just take *your* hair off and a little scalp with it?" he said to Buck. I was bent over laughing!

"Help," Buck pleaded. "Somebody please, help me." He sounded like a scared little boy.

"Let go of him," said Sheriff Ray Johnson, hitching his rifle. "And drop that knife, boy." Mr. Tucker and Papa were with him. Sky showed no fear of the sheriff or his gun.

"Do what he says, please," Papa pleaded. For his sake, Sky let Buck go and flipped the knife, which landed at the toe of Sheriff Johnson's left boot.

Buck scrambled to his feet, accusing Sky of jumping him and Jack. "That savage was going to scalp me," he said.

"They were going to cut his hair and Sky stopped them," I told the sheriff.

"Is that what happened?" the sheriff asked, looking at Buck, Jack, and Mr. Tucker. Neither one said anything. "I see," said the sheriff. "Let's go, then. Break it up," he told the Farley brothers. "Go on 'bout your business."

"I can't believe you gon' let this injun go on the

word of a nigra gal," said Jack. "This aine the way it 'sposed to be. We got to do something 'bout this."

"It's over for now," the sheriff answered. "Go on 'bout your business."

"Yeah," Jack said, grinning stupidly. "For now."

It was near dark when we got back home. A hoot owl called in the darkness. Sky frowned. "Something bad will happen before this night is over," he said.

"I dreamed of the prettiest wedding last night," said Mama, clicking her teeth. "A bad sign. Death is in the shadows."

Chapter 20

Buster let us know the night riders were coming long enough for us to get ready. We could see the torches glowing in the distance. A little after the westbound train to New Orleans passed through Quincy, a group of about fifteen Knights of the Southern Order of Manhood came riding into our yard, carrying torches, firing their guns wildly, and yelling.

I hurried down the loft ladder in my gown, no time to dress. Mama had told me that if the night riders ever came, I was to slip out the back window and run to the nearest black family and stay there until she or Papa came for me. But now that the Knights had finally come, I wasn't about to run. I was angry and ready to fight.

A spray of bullets shattered our front windows. The

shouts and yells grew louder. I could smell the odor of burning torches. Papa told Mama and me to stay under the big oak table. "Where is Sky, Papa? Do they have him?"

"Hard to see," he answered. "I don't think so."

I was sure the Knights had come for Sky — to tar and feather him, maybe hang him, the way they had done others for doing far less.

Papa took Sadie off the wall, even though there were no bullets in it. He pointed the barrel out the window, saying boldly, "Don't make me shoot one of you. You got no right coming here. . . ."

"You got no rights a white man is bound to honor," shouted one of the Knights. Their faces were covered, but they couldn't hide their voices. I recognized Mr. Charles Mayberry's voice.

"Anybody sell ammunition to that coon?" I recognized Buck Farley's voice and shuddered.

"I'm not giving you the boy, so it's best y'all go on, 'fore I have to shoot one of you."

There was laughter. "Burn the barn and torch the woods," one of them said. "We'll make an example out of this one. The others won't be so smart from now on. Then we'll go get that Jones boy. He won't be able to vote when we get through with him."

I crept to the far window of the kitchen where I could see clearly. This wasn't about Sky and the fight he'd had in town. This was about Papa making the desks and Lath Jones trying to vote.

Realizing now that he was the target, Papa burst out of the house and onto the porch facing his attackers, using Sadie as a club since it was empty. If Mama hadn't held me back, I'd been out there with him "Don't go near my barn," he yelled angrily.

"Shoot us," said one of the Knights, mocking Papa.

About that time the one going toward the barn with a torch let out a terrible yowl. His leg had been pierced by an arrow.

Zing! Another arrow grazed the ear of a Knight who cried out fearfully. "It's that injun. He's shooting arrows at us." It sounded like Mr. Tucker's voice.

"Anybody see where he is?"

Zing! An arrow went through a hood and zipped it off the head of a Knight. I got a good look at his face before he ducked back into the darkness.

Sky was placing the arrows right where he wanted

them, because he could have been deadly on target. The Knights seemed to know that, too, and some were ready to ride out. "Be men," one of the Knights said, throwing a torch in our window. Mama picked it up and hurled it back out the window.

Papa started after one of the Knights who was getting ready to throw a torch on the roof.

"Don't do it!" All eyes turned toward a man who had stepped from the shadows with Sky at his side. It was Mr. Wratten.

Confused and in disarray, the Knights of the Southern Order of Manhood scattered like a bunch of scared geese.

"They're gone! They're gone!" I said, rushing out the door to hug Papa and greet Mr. Wratten and Sky. But something was terribly wrong, I could see it in their faces. Then I heard a familiar whimper, a questioning sound. I looked down at the bottom of the porch steps. It was Buster! A stray bullet had hit him.

Chapter 21

Papa borrowed Mr. Wratten's horse and a loaded gun. "I've got to go warn my neighbor," he said. Sky wanted to go with Papa, but Mr. Wratten held him back. "Stop! Think. You can't afford to get involved in an incident." Mr. Wratten shifted to Apache. Sky answered with a nod. As best I could make out, Mr. Wratten was giving him a good tongue lashing about running away. Then his voice softened, and they greeted each other warmly.

Meanwhile Mama and I tried to help Buster. We had saved Buster's life once, but this time, all the finger crossing, hoping and praying and crying couldn't keep him alive. At last, Mama gave up. "Keep trying," I begged. "He's not really dead, just hurt bad."

"Daughter, listen to me. Buster is dead."

The words were so final. Death was forever.

I couldn't imagine never being able to hear Buster's curious yelps, to watch him chase a shadow not realizing it was his own tail, to feel his juicy licks on my hands and face, or to hug his body that was always moving, even when he was asleep. I figured that if I denied it long enough, he would spring to life and take off down the road scaring some poor critter . . . to death.

As the first rays of light touched his body and he made no move to greet the rising sun, I knew that Buster was really dead. When Papa got back, saying that the Joneses were okay for the time being, we wrapped Buster's body in a feed sack and buried him under the willow tree behind the house.

I felt like my soul had been dropped into a deep, dark hole, too, where there was no light or life. Mama chanted some old words she had learned from Grandma Jen. And Papa took me by the shoulders. "Buster wasn't useless," he said. "I was wrong about him." Sky said Apache words over Buster, then hurried away. It was his way.

I wanted to cry so bad, but I just couldn't anymore.

"You need to grieve," Mama said.

"I'll help fix breakfast," I said, quickly changing the subject.

Mr. Thompson and his three sons were the only workers to show up for work. The rest had been scared off by the Knights. I knew there was no danger that the Knights would come in the daylight hours. It wasn't their way.

As he passed the grits to Sky, Papa thanked Mr. Wratten for helping out against the Knights.

"I came here to bring the good news that Sky could stay with you," Mr. Wratten said matter-of-factly. Mama and I hugged each other, and Papa just grinned. But Mr. Wratten wasn't smiling. "Before you go getting all excited, I'm having second thoughts about him staying here. And, frankly, I'm worried. I mean, shooting white men with arrows could get Sky into real trouble.

"All the boy was doing was what anybody would do; he was defending his . . . his home," said Papa, pounding his fist on the table. "You saw what happened here. Those hood-wearing cowards came to stop me from making thirty desks. Sky helped to build those desks. Why shouldn't we have the right to defend our work, our home?"

Mr. Wratten looked at Papa with serious blue eyes. "Mr. Crossman, this is not about what's right and fair. All the Apaches were doing in Apacheria was defending their homes against people just like the Knights. But look at what happened to them. Why would I put Sky in the same situation when I know very well it's going to end up the same way?"

I wanted to jump in and say something, but I couldn't. Like I couldn't cry for Buster, I couldn't fight for Sky. I shoved the whole morning in a place far in the back of my head where I kept jealous and mean thoughts. What would we do without Sky? I thought.

"When I got your letter," Mr. Wratten went on, tossing two hot biscuits on his plate, "I read it to Geronimo first, before going to the superintendent with your request. When I finished, Geronimo asked to hold your letter, Mr. Crossman. After touching it for a few minutes, Geronimo gave it back to me, saying, 'Sky will be in a good place.' After that I had no trouble getting the superintendent's approval. But both of them gave me final say in the matter."

"And what do you say?" Papa asked directly.

"I don't know, yet," he answered, looking at Mama

and me. He asked Sky in Apache what he wanted to do. Sky answered he wanted to stay and learn from Papa, who was a good man and a fine maker of furniture.

"Who are these Knights?" Mr. Wratten asked, trying to make a decision he thought would be best for Sky and for us.

"Their whole purpose is to stop black people from making progress," Papa answered. "Afraid if we get a little business going, we won't be so willing to be sharecroppers."

"And the cowards wear hoods over their heads so we can't report them," Mama said, clicking her teeth in disgust. "But we know who they are. I caught a lot of their voices last night."

"I saw one of them," I said, remembering. "Sky shot one of the hoods off with an arrow, and I got a good look at one of the Knights."

Papa and Mr. Wratten agreed that we should go to town early the next morning and report what I'd seen. "I'd feel a whole lot better leaving Sky here if I knew those Knights were being handled by the authorities," said Mr. Wratten. I really didn't think it would do much good, but if my going could help Sky stay with us, I'd go. And on the chance that I might nail one of Buster's murderers, then I would gladly go.

After breakfast, Mr. Wratten took Sky aside. Although he told him in Apache, I understood enough to know that Lozen had died. Sky ran from the house and headed toward the woods. Just when you think it can't get any worse, it does.

"How did Lozen die?" I asked Mr. Wratten. He was surprised that I could speak Apache. "Sky is teaching me his language, but there are still sounds that are hard for me to make," I explained. "I far understand more than I can speak."

Mr. Wratten told me that Lozen had died of tuberculosis. I knew how much Sky admired her and her brother Victorio. It must have seemed all the people he looked up to were dead or dying. I couldn't explain it, but Lozen's death moved me, too. I hadn't known her up close, but I admired her courage, her strength, and her wisdom. Maybe I felt that way because Sky thought so much of her, and I thought so much of him. For whatever reason, I was sad that Lozen was no longer among the living.

Deciding that Sky should not be alone, I followed him to the cool, quiet woods. I found him down by the branch, Buster's favorite place. Sun glints filtered through the trees and flickered on the branch water like a thousand candles. Sky had built a small fire and was sitting, cross-legged and arrow straight into the flames, so still and stiff he seemed almost lifeless. I knew the fire was not for warmth because it was August, so I figured he was deep thinking, the way he did sometimes when he was sorting out things.

"*Shilahe,*" I said softly. "May I sit with you?"

He motioned for me to join him. I sat with my knees pulled up to my chin. Then, taking my hand in his, we sat looking into the fire, connected by our sorrow, our loss.

Just as I had learned to do, I silenced all the "whys" and "how comes" that were buzzing around in my head, and I let my eyes see into the flames. Soon the pictures came.

Through the smoke I saw Buster crashing out of the brush, nose to the ground, sniffing. In the flames I saw Buster lying at my feet, tail thumping, thumping. "Run free," I whispered. Then I saw the woman I had seen on the train, but younger now, running through a mountain pass, pointing the way the enemy was coming. It was Lozen, looking healthy and strong. "Run free," I whispered again. For all things there was a beginning and an end. Lozen and Buster had come to their end. So I had to let them go. And a wash of tears overtook me, and I shook with grief.

By the time the fire had died down, the sadness wasn't nearly so strong, and growing in its place was a powerful, peaceful feeling. Mama was right, as always. I needed to grieve. And once again Sky had helped me reach inside myself to find the strength I needed. "Can't you just imagine Buster," I said, wiping away the last of my tears. "He's probably having a good time chasing angels all over heaven." The idea made Sky smile.

He would not talk about Lozen. In fact, I never heard him mention her name again. That was his way. I never stopped telling Buster stories ever. That was my way.

Chapter 22

Just as planned, the following morning Papa, Mr. Wratten, and I rode into Quincy so I could tell about the Knight I had seen. Mama insisted that I wear my Sunday dress and she even tied satin ribbons on my braids, saying she wanted me to look like I belonged to somebody who cared. "Be particular," she said, "and hold your head up when you're talkin'."

Sky stayed at the house with Mama. Whatever Sky was thinking about Mr. Wratten's decision, he wasn't saying. But one thing I knew. If he wanted to run away again, I'd help him, sure.

The town looked deserted when we got there. It was the middle of the day, but many of the stores were closed. Odd thing for Mr. Tucker to close up, him being so tight about every penny. Where was the barber?

We pulled up in front of the courthouse and went into Sheriff Ray Johnson's office. He was seated behind his desk. Papa made a full report of everything that happened when the Knights had come to our farm. The sheriff listened real patient-like, nice as you please — almost syrupy nice.

"Well, Lee Andy, if you say their faces were covered, what can I do?" He shrugged. "Besides, you should have come to me long 'fore now."

"I saw one of them," I said.

He leaned forward. "What's his name?"

Suddenly I didn't feel so confident. I looked to Papa for support. He told me to go on. "I've never seen him before," I explained. "But I would know him if I ever saw him again."

The sheriff folded his arms and pushed back in his chair. He smiled. I thought how much he looked like a smiling hog. The picture of a big smiling hog made me want to laugh. But this was nothing to laugh about.

The sheriff made out like there was nothing he could do — not enough to go on. "The men who came to your farm are probably from another county. I can say for sure there are no Knights in this county." He took no more interest in anything else I had to say. Seemed more interested in who Mr. Wratten was than helping us.

"There's plenty you can do, sheriff," said Mr. Wratten, stepping forward.

"Now just who might you be?" the sheriff wanted to know.

"I'm with the United States Army," he said. "The Crossmans are part of a federal program over which I am in charge, sir." Mr. Wratten hadn't lied one bit, but he was making what he did sound much more important than it was. "I'm very concerned that nothing like this happens to these people again, otherwise it will have to be reported to higher authorities. You ever heard of the Ku Klux Klan Act? It outlaws organizations like the Knights of the Southern Order of Manhood. Anybody caught participating in one of these kinds of organizations is subject to federal prosecution."

Sheriff Ray Johnson assured us that he was going to look into the matter as soon as possible. "Lee Andy knows me," he said, eyes dancing about nervously.

"He's knows I'm fair to the coloreds. They voted me in. Didn't y'all?" And he gave us a piggish smile.

"I'm obliged for all you've done for me," said Papa. "But I heard the voices of those men. I know one was Tucker, and the Farley boys were there. We need protection."

The sheriff's eyes narrowed to slits. Now, he reminded me more of a snake than a pig. "You can't expect me to give you coloreds no special treatment. When you come to me with something solid to go on, I'll take care of things. But don't go accusing good citizens unless you're sure." The sheriff dismissed us, saying he had work to do.

When we reached the crossroads, Mr. Wratten turned north.

"You're not going back with us?" Papa asked, looking surprised. "What about Sky?"

"I've decided to let him stay. If in a few months things have stabilized in this community, then I'll think about letting him stay longer. Please believe me, I know how much you care for him and it's astonishing how much he had come to care about you. For that reason I am reluctant to take him away from you."

"You've been more than fair with us, Mr. Wratten. I appreciate everything you've done. Sky is like family. We'll do by him like we would any other kin."

They shook hands, and Mr. Wratten gave Papa the federal marshall's name in Mobile. "If you need help, go to Sam Peterson," he said. "Tell him you're a friend of mine. We served together as scouts. You can trust him. Meanwhile, I'll write to Sam myself—let him know what's going on here."

And with that said, Mr. Wratten tipped his hat, spurred his horse, and galloped away. "Did you hear that, Papa? Sky is getting to stay with us."

Papa patted me on the arm. "Darlin'," he said, "happy are them who wait on the Lord." It was one of his favorite sayings when something good had happened.

I couldn't wait to get home and tell Sky, when I realized I had lost one of my satin ribbons. Nothing for me to do but to go back to town. He hadn't gone far, but Papa fussed all the way back. Still, that was better than having to tell Mama that I'd lost part of the birthday present she'd given me.

After looking around outside the courthouse for the

lost ribbon, I went into Sheriff Ray Johnson's office. Seems I walked in on a meeting of the Knights of the Southern Order of Manhood. Sheriff Ray Johnson looked at me with cold piggish eyes as he limped over to his desk.

CHAPTER 23

Running, tripping, falling, I made my way out of the courthouse and to the wagon. Papa saw me coming and rushed to catch me as I stumbled down the uneven steps. Words tumbled out of my mouth, one on top of the other, as I tried to describe what I'd seen. "They're in there. All of them."

"Who? Where?"

Taking big gulps of air, I said, "The Farley brothers, Mr. Tucker, the owner of the hotel, the barber, even the man I saw — they're all sitting in Sheriff Ray Johnson's office."

Papa looked over his shoulder just in time to see the shutters in the sheriff's office open slightly. "They'd probably been meetin' when we came in, that's why all the shops are closed."

"The sheriff was limping!" I said. Mama was right not to trust him. "He's the one Sky hit in the leg with an arrow."

Papa slapped his hat against his leg. "All this time, he's been the snake at my heels," he said, "makin' a mockery of the law. Well, no more."

He marched straight into that snake pit, telling me to stay in the wagon. He should have known better. I waited a minute then followed him inside, ready to take on the Knights as well.

"Don't you go making on like this is something illegal," said Sheriff Ray Johnson. "We're having a town business meeting."

I watched their faces as Papa told them, "I know who you are, and I plan to report you all." Their eyes were filled with anger and hatred. Why did they hate us so much?

"It's yo' word 'gainst ours," one of the Knights yelled out.

"If you got plans to hurt me or mine, just remember that George Wratten is going to make a full report of this to the federal marshal's office in Mobile," Papa said, his voice shaking with emotion. "If anything happens to me, my family, my timber, my farm, or my mule, they'll be comin' after you. Now go tell that to Mr. Mayberry. Tell him he can't have everything all the time! The real law is on our side."

"Not for long," Mr. Tucker hissed. "We're changing the laws every day to keep this country free for white people."

"We gon' take the right to vote out of yo' hands," said Sheriff Ray Johnson, showing his real face. The one he showed us had been a mask. "Aine right that we whites have to be beholden to a bunch of nigra voters."

"Do what you may," said Papa, "but come this election day, I'll still have the vote and I won't be votin' for you." Then he walked out, closing the door on the sheriff and the rest of the Knights.

CHAPTER 24

Papa had stood toe-to-toe with the Knights and was still around to tell about it. Naturally we were a little bit proud and a little bit scared. But nobody could have looked up to Papa more than Sky. "It is an honor to stand with you, Mr. Lee Andy," Sky told Papa when he found out he'd be staying with us. "It is good to be in your home, Miz Georgianne," Sky said to Mama. "And Little Bush, it makes me happy to be your brother."

As happy as we all were, none of us was surprised when, by week's end, Sheriff Ray Johnson called in the note he'd been holding at Tucker's General Store for Papa's seeds and supplies. The bill was three times as high as it should have been, but even after Mama had checked all the figures everything seemed in order, nothing that could be called illegal in a court of law. Papa had to settle the debt in thirty days or lose the farm.

None of the men who promised to help showed up for work, except Mr. Thompson and his boys. Couldn't blame them too much. Papa put the Thompsons to work sawing and planing the wood. But not one desk had been started. On Friday, I heard Papa tell Mr. Thompson that he wouldn't be needing him anymore because he was going to send back the advance money Mr. Washington had sent.

"Why don't you use that money to pay off your debt, buy yourself some time," said Mr. Thompson. I waited for Papa's answer.

"That's not the way good business is done," he said. "Doin' wrong can't make a right." How many times had I heard Papa say that without really understanding how hard it was to be true to what you believed. "If we start off doin' wrong, we'll be just like the Un-people Jane's always talkin' 'bout. We'll be undoing all the rest of our unhappy lives." So Papa did listen to me. Sky admired Papa because of what Papa did. I loved Papa because of what he didn't do.

Before sending the money back, Mr. Thompson

begged Papa to speak to the men once more. "A lot of them were just plain scared of the Knights and what they might do. But, if you tell them about the federal marshals and all, I bet they'll come back to work."

Well, come Sunday, when service was over and meetings were sometimes held, Papa put his problem before the church members, then he called for their support. "I got less than thirty days to build thirty desks and save my farm. I sure could use your help."

Some of the men who had promised to help but hadn't were too ashamed to look at Papa straight in the face. Embarrassed, I guess. Those who looked, though, saw a weary man. My father had aged right before my eyes. The weight of our troubles had put a slight bend in his back, and it made him look like a traveler who had walked too far without rest. In that moment, I realized why Mama had been so frightened when the boll weevils had gotten the cotton. I wanted to run, too. I wanted to beg him to leave this place, run away, far away, maybe take Sky back to the Southwest.

Then I remembered my loft, Mam's sweet humming at the fireplace, Papa sanding a piece of wood, and Sky sitting in front of his *wickiup,* chanting to the rising of the sun, and I knew why we shouldn't leave. Before I knew it, I was on my feet. "May I say something, please?"

A hush fell over the congregation. Children were to be seen, but never heard. But I was determined, even if it meant my legs would get switched when I got home. "Suffer the little ones to come," said Reverend Henry, extending his hand for me to come up and speak.

"My father is a good man. He doesn't steal, cheat, or lie." I swallowed, all the time hoping and praying that sensible words would come to me. "The farm he's trying so hard to save is our special spot here on his earth. You have a spot like that, too. Most of us call it home. I think your home is worth fighting for, even if you lose." And I sat down.

"Oh, and a child shall lead us," said Reverend Henry, giving me a big hug. By the look on Mama's face, I wasn't in too much trouble.

"I reckon tomorrow morning I'll be at your place," said Lath Jones. Mama patted Miz Annie's hand. We were all relieved to see that the Joneses were doing well. They had hidden out among friends after the Knight attack, but they were back at their home now. Mr. Jones wasn't likely to take low to anybody.

By the time we left church Papa had close to twelve workers, not nearly as many as he needed to finish the desks, not in thirty days. But Papa had decided to go as far as he could, then wait on the Lord.

Work began at can see and didn't end until can't see. Since Mama knew figuring, Papa put her in charge of the money. I helped by toting water and fetching things and doing my regular chores. And of course, Sky was always at Papa's side, cutting, sanding, polishing. Sometimes in the evening we went hunting. Both Papa and I were getting pretty good with the bow and arrows Sky had made for us.

The Knights of the Southern Order of Manhood didn't ride on us again, but things got real hard for Papa in town. Mr. Tucker claimed he didn't have whatever Papa needed in his store, yet it was in clear view. "Sold to somebody else," he said. So Papa had to ride miles away to get the supplies or wire Mr. Washington to send it to him from Tuskegee.

The first week of September was hotter than any we had in July or August. Papa and Sky began work in the early morning hours when it was cooler. Then they took off during the heat of the day and picked up again, working deep into the night. Papa's spirits ran high, even though it was plain to see the work was going very slowly.

"He's got to have help," Sky told me. "We will never finish all those desks on time."

Chapter 25

Papa and Mama thought the worst when we came home from church one Sunday and found Sky gone.

"I don't know what he's doing but I'll bet he's trying to help," I said, unwilling to believe the worst of my friend, my brother. "Just you wait and see." I was so sure, I must have convinced them.

Sky didn't let us down either. A few days later, he and Mr. Wratten came riding up the road with two wagons full of Apaches, men and women, and four guards. They had come to help build the desks.

Right away the women began building wickiups in the plowed-over field. By nightfall, campfires glowed in the darkness. "Aren't you afraid of the Apaches running away?" I asked Mr. Wratten.

"Running away to live among the '*Indaa* is not considered an improvement for most Apaches. To leave the group is to trade an almost sure death amongst friends and relatives for an almost sure death amongst strangers. That Sky ran away is amazing enough but his attachment to your family is even more unusual, very special indeed."

"Once again, I'm in your debt," Papa said, shaking George Wratten's hand.

"Not me you should thank," he said. "The superintendent is always looking for ways to counteract the boredom at Mount Vernon, so he wasn't hard to convince that a work project like this one would be helpful, but it had to be all volunteers. Sky is the one who told his people that you needed help. They are here out of respect for Sky, who presented his case well."

"Besides, they were bored to death at Mount Vernon and welcomed the chance to get away," Sky put in.

I was so glad to have my brother back home, I was sputtering with excitement, asking questions and without waiting for an answer hurling another one at him. I was talking so much and so fast, some of the

Apaches looked at Sky with wonder in their eyes, shook their heads, and walked away. "They think I talk too much, don't they?" I whispered to Sky. He smiled and didn't answer, which was his way.

Over the next few days more and more people showed up for work. Papa had more workers than he needed. The wives came, too, bringing food and a willingness to help. It was something to see, the black women from our community and the Apache women all cooking together, sharing a pinch of this and a dash of that, which gave old recipes a new twang. There was always a big pot of something bubbling under the ramada put together from the garden, the orchard, army rations, and wild game the men had caught. Although the soldiers brought their own rations, when they smelled all that good cooking, they put the rations in Mama's hands and they ate with us, too.

Mama was a bridge between the two worlds of women, moving comfortably between them. When the awful burden was lifted off Papa's shoulders, he seemed to step a little higher, smile a little faster. Lying in my loft, I dared to let myself feel safe again.

During the day our farm was a bustling, busy place, where desks were being made. Seeing Sky with his own people, watching him talking, sharing, made me look at him in a new way. Even though he was still very young, he had earned his people's respect. He was a person worthy of their honor. He and Mr. Wratten did most of the translating and I helped out at the ramada best I could. The Apache women laughed when I tried to say something was hot and instead I said it was rotten. Not at all what I meant. There were certain Apache words I just couldn't make with my tongue.

Although our black neighbors went to their homes and returned each morning, the guards made their beds in the barn, but the Apaches went out to their *wickiups*. I could hear them sometimes from my loft window, telling old, old stories about the first Apaches who were strong, brave, and wise. Sometimes before I fell asleep, I heard Mama singing an old spiritual, followed by an Apache singing a lovely lullaby. This is the way the Garden of Eden must have been before Un-people came into the world, I thought.

Not a moment too soon the desks were completed with three days left before the end of the month. Papa and Mr. Wratten rode into town to meet with Sheriff

Ray Johnson regarding the debt. Mr. Wratten vouched that Papa had earned the money and would be paying his debt. Sheriff Johnson had no choice but to agree.

Papa wasn't one to poke fun at anybody, but he got a kick out of showing us how Sheriff Ray Johnson's face looked when he found out Papa had the money to pay him. It didn't take much imagination for me to see the sheriff's piggish face all twisted with unkindness.

Mr. Wratten announced that he and the Apaches were pulling out the next morning. It was Mama's idea to have a big party. "No work, just lots of fun."

Way in the night when we had danced until our feet were sore, and we had stuffed ourselves with fried rabbit with gravy, rice, stewed tomatoes, apples, corn, squash, and cornbread, I drifted off to sleep, thinking that the Apaches' going was bound to leave a big hole in the material of my life.

When I woke the next morning, the Apaches had broken camp and loaded their things in the wagons. We had come to know Sky's people and even though we had very different ways, we learned from each other and shared food and ideas. And somehow by our working together we had managed to make something good happen.

I would miss them, even the guards who at first didn't seem to care about any of us at first. But before pulling away, they presented Mama with a pretty blue scarf, saying, "This is for you, Miz Georgianne, for helping turn our army rations into real food. Caine everybody do tha."

After tearful good-byes and promises to visit, the wagons pulled away. I stood at the road, waving until they were all the way out of sight, feeling happy and sad. Sad that my friends were gone, but happy that I had gotten to know them all.

On Christmas Eve Papa learned that Mr. Washington was ordering thirty more desks. He had handled his business well, according to Mr. Washington's letter of appreciation. Papa'd completed the job in record time, paid his workers, including the Apaches, and all his debtors. "Happy are those who wait on the Lord," Papa said, placing the letter in his Bible.

"You always saying that, Lee Andy," Mama said, stirring a skillet of corn and tomatoes she'd learned to cook from the Apaches.

" 'Cause it's true."

Mama was full of mischief. She winked at me. "You can wait all you want to," Mama put in, stirring a pot, "but when the Lord comes I plan to be busy doing something."

Papa headed straight for the barn.

Sky and I sat out under the full moon, huddled under one of Mama's quilts. "Are you glad Mr. Wratten said you could stay with us as long as you wanted?"

"Yes," he answered quickly. Coming from Sky that meant he was very glad, and I smiled.

"How long will that be?"

He didn't answer. I looked up at the winter trees that looked like black lace against the gray velvet darkness. Sky didn't talk much in the winter or tell many stories. He tended to be somber and quieter than usual. I thought at first he was missing his people, then I realized it was the time of Ghost Face, a time not to disturb the dark spirits. But I kept after him until he agreed to learn a few Christmas carols. He especially liked "Silent Night."

Mama made magic in the kitchen on Christmas Day, turning ordinary food into a feast — turkey, dressing, and sweet potatoes, okra, and cabbage, crowder peas, and of course corn pudding for Sky.

"Ooooh, Sky," I said, teasing, "you're eating turkey! Next you'll be eating fish. Or maybe a pork chop!"

"Never," he said. And we all laughed.

While my folks exchanged gifts and talked and laughed about old times, Sky beckoned for me to follow him. "Got something for you, Little Bush."

He led me to the spot where I had found him months ago, sick and feverish. So much had happened since then. Somewhere in the darkness, I heard a familiar sound. "Buster," I said, looking closer. No. There lying in the straw was a puppy that looked just like Buster. He had the same huge feet, the same redbone coloring, and a tail that could not be still, and swished from side to side. I picked him up in my arms and buried my face in his fur. He was an armful of happy whimperings and wiggles.

"Wiggles," I said, naming him. I fell backward into the straw and let him climb all over me, sniffing, licking my face. "Where'd you find him?" I asked.

"One of the Thompson boys told me that Buster

had sired some pups with their dog. He let me have this one because he said it was untrainable. Too wild. Useless!"

"That makes him perfect, then," I said. "Just perfect."